Rachel Billington writes, 'Ruby and Slate are born and bred in the city to hard pavements, noisy roads, tall buildings, crowded shops and classrooms. I've lived in London since I was five but I always had an escape route. The best of all was an island off the coast of Ireland where I spent many holidays. It gave me time to breathe and dream. At the front sheep grazed and a small aeroplane once landed on the smooth grass. But the back was a wild place, with steep cliffs and strange noises and unexplored hills and caverns. That island is the inspiration for *Far Out!*'

Rachel was the fifth of eight brothers and sisters and has four children herself. She has published 16 adult novels, the most recent of which is *A Woman's Life*, and 7 children's books. Until recently she was president of the writers' organisation PEN. She is also co-editor of the only national newspaper for prisoners, *Inside Time*. She spends part of her time in Dorset and part in London.

Other titles available from Hodder Children's Books:

Far Out!

RACHEL BILLINGTON

Hodder
Children's
Books

A division of Hodder Headline Limited

A Catalogue record for this book is available from
the British Library

ISBN 0 340 85477 4

Typeset by Avon Dataset Ltd, Bidford-on-Avon, Warks

Printed and bound in Great Britain by
Bookmarque

Hodder Children's Books
A division of Hodder Headline Limited
338 Euston Road
London NW1 3BH

For Phineas and Raphael

Contents

CHAPTER ONE

Audition for Life

The card was pinned up on the school notice board. Ruby spotted it at once because it was such a weird shape. She tried to describe it to her friend, Lee. 'It was more like a hole than a card, as if someone had poked right through the board.'

'What was more like a hole?' Lee was making fun as usual.

'The card. The new notice.'

'What notice?'

'It was a kind of funny colour, too, like very dark but with swirly colours . . .' She stopped abruptly at the look on Lee's face. 'You must have seen it. It said "Audition

1

for Life, ring 07248 . . ." Well, I can't remember the rest. It was a long number, probably a mobile.'

'Ruu-bee, try not to be as stu-pid as you are.' Lee started to walk away. 'There was no card that looked like a hole with swirly colours though very dark too. I stood in front of the notice board for just as long as you and the only new card said, "Found, one red fountain pen without top and one black shoe requiring mending". You should get stronger glasses.'

'I'll show you!' Ruby grabbed Lee's arm and tried to drag her back down the corridor.

'And be late for Miss Killer King. No thank you!'

'But in break it might not be there.'

'It never *was* there, blind girl.'

Dismally, Ruby gave up the argument and followed Lee. She supposed that was why she was her special friend, because she always knew better about everything. Nevertheless, she promised herself that at the end of the day she'd sneak another look at the notice board. She couldn't really have imagined that strange-looking card. Or could she?

It was quite dark in the corridor when Ruby got back to the notice board. Most of the lights had already been turned off and, since it was February, there was not much light coming from outside either. So Ruby didn't see the boy dressed all in black, anorak over dark trousers, until she was nearly up to him. He called himself Slate and moved in the kind of cool crowd even Lee didn't dare

2

talk to. Now he was frowning considerably, his brows crossing above his nose. Ruby was about to creep away when he crooked his finger.

'Hey, you! Didn't I see you like standing here earlier?'

'Uhuh. Yes. I think.'

'Did you see pinned up here, a like strange coloured card, irregular outline, sort of a hole?'

'Yes! Yes!' cried Ruby. ' "An Audition for Life".' She felt her glasses sliding down her nose in her excitement and pushed them up firmly. So someone else had seen the card, which meant she was not so 'stu-pid' after all.

'Audition for what?' Slate came closer. 'Say again.'

'Audition for Life.' Nervous, Ruby found herself rattling on. 'That's what it said. But I didn't get the number. It was very long and I've no head for numbers. Not above five if you know what I mean . . .'

'I got the numbers.' Ruby was surprised to see Slate looking at her with respect. 'I'm good with numbers, but I didn't get the words. I guess we're different kinds of people. Or, to put it another way round, we work well together.'

'Oh, do we really,' breathed Ruby humbly.

'So when do we make the call?' As Slate spoke, he pulled a purple mobile from his jacket pocket, which dislodged several Pokémon cards. He stuffed them back hastily; they were forbidden in school.

Everything was going too fast for Ruby. She looked round nervously. 'We might get locked in if we stay here much longer.'

'Check. I need to get my things. Let's meet on Orchard Street in ten minutes.'

This wasn't like real life, thought Ruby as she watched Slate speed away. She heaved her own tattered bag on to her shoulder.

Outside the gates, she was immediately pounced on by Lee. 'Where've you been? Who were you with? Didn't I see you with someone?'

'Nothing. I mean no one. I've got to go.' After Lee's mocking refusal to admit there ever was that weird card, Ruby certainly didn't want her to come along to Orchard Street. This was her special adventure. 'I've got to go,' she repeated. 'My mum needs me back early,' she lied. Her mother was never home before six thirty.

'Oh, if that's how you feel.' And Lee stamped off down the road. Soon she had joined a group of girls and they all began giggling and looking back at where Ruby stood on her own. She tried to appear bold and defiant as she set off for Orchard Street, which luckily was on her way home so it wouldn't seem as if she were lying, but inside she worried whether it was worth the risk of losing her one and only friend, for the sake of what? She had no idea.

'Hi. You were longer than ten minutes.' Slate stood in a kind of confident slouch, one hand in his pocket, the other holding his mobile.

'Sorry. I had to shake off a friend.'

'Stellar. Like who's going to speak?'

'You!' exclaimed Ruby, amazed he should even ask.

'I dunno.' Slate looked down and scuffed his toe on the pavement. 'You've got a better voice than me.'

'What?'

'Kind of clever sounding.' It was true that Slate slurred his words together so sometimes Ruby missed part of his sentences but she had admired this as a sign of cool. 'You know something funny,' continued Slate as Ruby dithered. 'None of my mates saw that card. Not one. If I hadn't met you I would have thought I'd been seeing things.'

'Me too,' said Ruby. 'My friend did think I was seeing things.'

'So who's going to make this call then?'

They were standing under a lamp post which must have been broken because up till then it had been dark, but all of a sudden it switched itself on and, by its new alarming light, Ruby suddenly realised that big, cool Slate was afraid of making the call. 'OK,' she said. 'I'll do it. But you put the numbers in first.'

'Check.' Carefully, he punched them in.

Ruby held the phone, which was warm and seemed to vibrate as if it were alive. It rang so many times that her heart, which had been thudding fit to burst, had calmed down a little by the time a voice said, 'Audition for Life. This is Cherie speaking.' It was a woman's voice, warm but very brisk. 'You now have five options: for Tragedy press one, for Comedy press two, for Song press three, for Dance press four. For all four, press five. You have ten seconds to make your decision.'

'It's a recorded message. We've got ten seconds to decide.' Ruby spoke as fast as she could. 'Tragedy, comedy, song or dance or all of them?' They stared at each other desperately and might never have made up their minds if Ruby's finger hadn't slipped on to number five.

'You have chosen correctly,' said Cherie's voice, sounding a little more relaxed. 'You now have three further options: City, Country, Island. For City, press one, for Country press two, for Island three.'

'Island!' shouted Slate and Ruby together. Though they'd never thought of it before, they were both thoroughly sick of the city, and the country (which they hardly knew) made them think of rain and large, dirty and possibly angry animals.

'Well done,' pronounced the voice encouragingly after Ruby had pressed number three. 'You may now attend the first available auditions in your area, which will be on February 29th at five o'clock in the Salvation Army hall on Mountjoy Street. Frederick and April Whipple, co-founders of The Audition for Life, will look forward to meeting you. Please bring a hat, a bucket, a pet animal.' The message clicked off.

Desperate not to forget any of it, Ruby gabbled it off to Slate without taking in what she was saying.

'This is fly!' His face said it all. 'February 29th's that leap year thing. Only comes once every four years. And you tell me if you've ever heard of a Salvation Army hall on Mountjoy Street?'

'I don't know Mountjoy Street,' said Ruby, a little sharply because she had just taken in the bit about a pet and her mother disliked animals so much she wasn't even allowed to *talk* about other people's pets, let alone have one herself. 'We'll just have to think about it,' she added weakly.

'Yeah. Well, think about it till tomorrow,' said Slate, picking up his bag and putting his mobile away. 'But if you're low on pets, I can give you a choice of pigeons, dogs, cats, gerbils, rabbits, mice, stick insects and snakes. Well, one snake. No choice.'

'Wicked,' Ruby said faintly.

'My big brother's crazy about animals. He's sort of crazy, full stop. He collects animals to sell but then he never sells them. See ya.'

He was off, striding down the dark road, leaving Ruby where she was until, just before he turned the corner, she got herself together enough to shout, 'We are going to audition, aren't we?'

' 'Course we are.' He turned to her for a moment and then was gone.

Chapter Two

Ruby meets a dove and a snake

The next morning Ruby's mother was surprised to find her daughter poring over a map of the city. 'What's got into you now, Ruby? Aren't your eyes bad enough without straining them over street plans?' Mrs Gutch already had her coat on and her head poised on one side as she screwed in her second earring. 'And do try to grow some more inches today. People will think there's something wrong with the way I feed you if you stay so small.'

Ignoring this remark because she'd heard it so often and long ago decided there was nothing she could do to make herself grow, Ruby followed Mrs Gutch to the door. 'Do you know where Mountjoy Street is?'

'Nasty run-down area. Now don't make me late. We're short of a junior today.' She shut the door in Ruby's face before opening it again for one last piece of advice. 'And do tie your hair back or you'll be taken for a burning bush and no one will believe I'm a hairdresser.'

Ruby thought she could do no more about her red, frizzy hair than she could about her height, so, ignoring this bit of advice too, she carefully inserted the map in her bag and set off for school. With any luck, Slate's sharp eyes would spot Mountjoy Street.

But the morning passed and Ruby only saw Slate in the distance, surrounded by his usual gang of cool friends. She would never dare approach him and, since he was the year above, they wouldn't meet in class.

'What's got into you? You look even more pathetic than usual.' Lee swung around on her long legs.

'Thanks for nothing.' It was the lunch break. Usually, they swapped sandwiches but, as Lee hadn't spoken to her so far, Ruby was already eating hers.

'Come on, you must have more than one little cheese bun. Let's see what's in your bag.'

Before Ruby could protest, she delved into the bag and pulled out the map. 'Hey, what's this? You going exploring or something?'

Suddenly Ruby felt near tears and knew she had to talk to someone. 'No. It's about the card I saw yesterday. Slate saw it too and we're going to audition in the Salvation Army hall in Mountjoy Street but Slate won't speak to me and I can't find Mountjoy Street.' To her shame, she felt tears brim over her eyes and run down her cheeks.

'I see,' said Lee. And at least she wasn't using that horrid mocking voice. 'Well, I wouldn't trust Slate as far as I could throw him, but I know where Mountjoy Street is.'

'You do?' In a moment, Ruby's tears vanished.

'I'm not telling, though. Not if it means you're going off with that rude Slate boy, a year older than you too! What would your mum think of him?'

'She wouldn't think anything,' cried Ruby desperately. 'You wouldn't tell her, would you? He's no different to you and me.'

'He's a boy and he's not nice like you and me.'

Ruby knew Lee was winding her up just for the fun of it, but she didn't want to run away if Lee really did know where Mountjoy Street was. And she wasn't altogether wrong about her mother, who disapproved of boys nearly as much as she disapproved of men. 'If you tell me where it is, I'll buy you that toe ring you like.'

Lee sighed as if she could take or leave such a pathetic offer. 'My cousin used to work in Mountjoy Street,' she said in a bored voice. 'It's just off Market Square. Past the old swimming pool. It's a horrid street. That's why she left.'

'But is there a Salvation Army hall there?'

'Not that I ever saw.' Lee's attention seemed to be directed over Ruby's shoulder and, turning round, she saw Slate approaching down the corridor. He was on his own, chewing gum in a laconic way. 'Now see if he speaks to you,' whispered Lee.

Both girls watched silently. Slate had almost passed before he muttered out of the side of his mouth (the other half was filled with gum), 'Orchard Street, sixteen ten hours.' Then he had gone.

Ruby found herself blushing under Lee's accusing stare. 'What did he say?'

'We're going to meet later . . .' Before Ruby could finish her sentence, Lee had flounced away.

'You're so stu-pid!' she shouted over her shoulder. And, rather miserably, Ruby thought she probably was. 'And don't forget the toe ring!' As if she'd be allowed to. She waved at Lee and walked away wondering what chance there was, even if they found this Salvation Army hall, that she'd pass an audition which involved singing and dancing. None. Less than none.

'Hey, what hit you on the head?' Slate greeted her, just as the lamp post burst into life. Wearily, Ruby set down her bag. Her doubts about the whole mad project made her bolder and crosser.

'Why don't you ever speak to me? It makes me feel stupid.'

Slate seemed surprised. 'Cool it. Of course I can't speak to you in school. This is our secret, isn't it? Do you want to let the whole world know what we're up to?'

Guiltily, Ruby remembered her tearful outburst to Lee. 'No. No, of course not.' It was on the tip of her tongue to tell him the whole idea of an audition filled her with terror, when he grabbed her arm.

'Come on then. I'm taking you to my place to choose a pet.' Slate seemed in high spirits as he led her along the streets. Soon they were in an area she didn't know, where the few houses were squeezed between high-rise blocks and open spaces blew with plastic bags and empty cans. 'Don't worry,' said Slate, cheerfully. 'We're nearly there. Our street got left behind when they knocked down the rest. My granddad was such an iron man, he faced off the diggers single-handed.'

'Oh,' said Ruby. 'My granddad retired to Walthamstow. He gardens, I think.'

'We've got a garden but it's filled with animals.'

The house they had stopped in front of would have been quite pretty, Ruby thought, if it hadn't been surrounded by a wire fence towering above her head and wound about with barbed wire.

'We'll go round the side.'

'Wow!' exclaimed Ruby, which was an understatement as she found herself facing four of the biggest dogs she'd ever seen. This had become an adventure already.

'The Spice Girls. Ha!' introduced Slate. 'Notice they're tethered. We'll go on inside. One wolfhound, one Great Dane, one German shepherd and one mix of all three. She was one of Brent's failures. Brent!' shouted Slate. 'Not here,' he replied himself.

Now they were inside the house in a room filled with cats. 'The Beatles,' said Slate, indifferently. 'Brent's very lazy with names. Do you want to see the snake now, the mice or the pigeons? Or maybe they're doves.'

'The pigeons,' said Ruby, hastily. 'Or doves. Really I should go home.'

'Home? I've got food in, if you're hungry.'

'Do you have any parents?' she asked. They had arrived in a kitchen, which seemed fairly normal until she noticed the ceiling was very low because several feet from the ceiling downwards were used as a cage for pigeons or doves. They were cooing now in a very sweet way.

'Mum died. Dad's away a lot. Travelling.' Slate answered her question nonchalantly as he stood on the table and, reaching above him, took out a white bird, which he stroked gently. 'Aurora,' he said, stepping down. 'I called her that. She's tame. Here, you take her.'

Thinking how shocked her mother would be, Ruby took the bird gingerly. 'She's so soft.'

'That's you fixed, then. We'll put a bit of string on her. Are you sure you don't want to see the snake? He has a name too. He's called Hannibal the Cannibal. Only teasing. His real name's Blackadder.' Slate laughed uproariously at his own joke. 'Actually he's called Cedric.'

Frowning crossly, Ruby handed him Aurora. 'I don't think you're a very nice person. It's quite natural to be frightened of snakes. You're the odd one.' It struck Ruby that when she was with Slate she was quite outspoken, not like her usual mousey self at all, although that might be because there was so much to be outspoken about.

'Have it your own way. Perhaps I'll ask Brent for a new animal.'

'I've got to go.' She really did, she realised suddenly. If she arrived back after her mother, she'd have to lie and Ruby tried to avoid lying, partly because she was bad at it.

'Take these crisps, anyway.' Slate let her out past the dogs who looked hungrily at the crisp packet. 'See you at the bus stop tomorrow. And don't forget a hat and bucket.'

Ruby was hurrying down the road, nervously trying to avoid looking at the high-rises with the wind whistling when she remembered they didn't know where to find the hall. Nevertheless, she realized, rather to her surprise that, despite all her anxieties, she was looking forward to continuing the adventure tomorrow. It was as if that card and knowing Slate had opened a whole new world for her.

Chapter Three

The 111 bus stop

'What've you got in your bag now?' Lee sidled up to Ruby suspiciously. 'It's full to bursting.'

Ruby tried not to smile. What would Lee think if she told her she had one red and green plastic bucket from the seaside and one flowery bath hat belonging to her mother, who was very particular about not getting her hair wet because it dried even more frizzy than usual.

'Nothing,' she said firmly.

'I expect you've still got that map?' Ruby kept quiet. 'Anyway you'll never find your Salvation Army hall because I asked my mum and she said it was knocked down when she was my age.' Giving Ruby a push – it was only a push because their school was very firm on violence between pupils – Lee scooted off to the playground. At least she'd forgotten to ask for her toe ring.

It was a cold clear day with no sign of rain, which Ruby thought quite a relief if she and Slate were to wander around looking for a hall that didn't exist. As on the day before, Slate didn't come near her all day, except just at the end when he appeared for a moment at her side, 'See you at the 111 bus stop. Sixteen thirty hours. I've got to pick up the pets first.'

He had gone before Ruby could ask him where the 111 bus stop was.

Perhaps I'm not cut out for adventure after all, thought Ruby dismally as she stood at the bus stop – at least she had found that – I am too cowardly, too stupid and too small. Ruby knew why she was small. It was because she had been born two months earlier than expected, weighing only as much as a cabbage, as her mother put it. In her mother's mind (which she had told Ruby once every few weeks for as long as she could remember), her unexpected early birth and the months of hospital visits while she lay looking ugly in an incubator had driven off her father, never to be seen again.

'He couldn't bear not being the centre of attention,' Mrs Gutch liked to explain to her friends. 'He called Ruby "the little worm" you know, and when he discovered I couldn't have any more children because of what her birth had done to me, that was it!'

Ruby had long ago decided she wouldn't have wanted a father who called her a little worm, although she had to admit that sometimes, like now, she felt very worm-like indeed. Looking up, a large raindrop sploshed into her eye.

'Go on, love,' said a fat woman, pushing her from behind. 'Either get on the bus or get out of the way.'

'Sorry, I'm waiting for . . .' but just at that moment, Slate came racing out of nowhere and she found herself propelled on to the bus. He was heavily laden with a large tin bucket, a backpack and a wire basket, so their entry was not welcomed.

'This isn't a removal van, you know,' was the politest comment.

Slate ignored all this. 'Ten stops,' he panted as they stood together in the crowded bus and, from the cage, Ruby heard the soothing murmur of a dove cooing.

'Off!' Ruby looked at Slate, pushing her out of the bus as he had pushed her in and decided he wasn't very good at words. She wondered if he thought in words or only in pictures of action. On the other hand, without all his pushing and shoving, she'd probably have run away ages ago.

They stood on Mountjoy Street, in sudden streaming rain. The pigeon stopped cooing. 'Did you bring a snake in the end?' asked Ruby, but Slate only muttered something she couldn't hear. As he seemed unsure what

17

to do next, she continued, 'There was a hall here once so maybe it was rebuilt. At least it's not a very long street.'

They could see the beginning and the end from where they stood; most of it taken up by the sort of shops that don't bother to put anything very nice in the window and get protective shutters up as soon as they close. Some of them were closed already. 'We could ask someone,' she suggested.

'Hate asking people,' Slate started to walk away so that Ruby had no choice but to follow him.

Half an hour later, she was still following him, wet through, cold, exhausted and very anxious. They had struggled up and down the street three times; all the shops had closed except one, a newsagent which they now stood in front of. 'I'm going in,' announced Ruby as Slate turned his back.

The shop was very small and seemed even smaller because it was stuffed full with anything anyone could ever want to buy including, Ruby happened to notice, a surprising amount of buckets and hats. 'Sorry to bother you,' she began in her politest voice, 'but we're looking for the Salvation . . .' Before she could finish, the man behind the counter – he was so bent over a book she could hardly see his face – answered. 'Blue door to the left.'

Triumphantly, Ruby rushed out to Slate. 'Blue door to the left!' she repeated.

'We're looking for a hall, not a door,' grumbled Slate.

Ruby wasn't allowing him to get away with that. 'Perhaps that's why we missed it,' she said firmly.

Back they went up the street again and it was Slate who eventually found the door, blue with a crumbly stone arch, half-covered with ivy.

'No wonder we missed it,' said Ruby, trying not to shiver with a mixture of cold and excitement. 'It's not a door in a building. It's a door to somewhere else!'

'Let's hope it's not locked.'

It was not locked but what they found the other side was not very cheering. Brambles, straggling creepers, stumps of half-dead bushes garlanded by old bits of paper and worse, blocked their way.

'It's a dump,' said Slate.

'It's Sleeping Beauty's palace,' said Ruby, more romantically, keeping her eyes firmly on the brambles. 'Anyway, it has to lead somewhere or it wouldn't be here. I mean you wouldn't have a fine door and an arch like that to a dump.' She thought that, even if she was small and puny, just at the moment she seemed to have more determination than Slate.

'Have it your way.' Putting down his packages and picking up a stick, he began to beat at the biggest obstructions in their path. Inch by inch, they made their way along. Beyond the tangle of plants, there were high brick walls on either side so that it was very dark, with the only light coming from a full moon which was shining straight ahead of them. At least the rain was less heavy.

'I told mum I was going round to Lee's,' said Ruby, wanting to hear the sound of a human voice. 'Will anyone worry about you?'

'I look after myself,' said Slate tersely.

Suddenly, Ruby realised that there had been no big shrubs to knock out of their way for several minutes and that there was something extremely solid ahead of them which just might be—

'The hall!' she cried.

They approached it warily, as you might stalk a wild animal, not quite certain if it would disappear back into the jungle. Soon they could make out a wide doorway rising to a pointed spire and two arched windows on either side.

'It's a church!' exclaimed Slate, once more setting down his bucket and cage.

'Salvation Army halls always look like churches,' said Ruby who, although she had never seen one before, vaguely connected them to God. What was worrying her far more was that there was no sign of life, no jolly noises, no lights in the window. In fact, since the sound of traffic has receded to somewhere far away, she had never been in such a silent place in her life.

'Now we're here, we'd better go in . . .' Slate seemed about to run at the door.

'Hold on a minute,' Ruby tried to think of some delaying tactic. 'Shouldn't we put on our hats and get ready our buckets and pets?'

'Huh!' Under Slate's scornful eyes, Ruby got out her

mother's bath hat into which she crammed as much of her wild red frizz as she could fit.

'I wish I'd thought of it before the rain got at my hair.' She turned to Slate but, instead of smiling as she'd expected, he was staring at her with horror.

'I'm not going in with you like that. You'd make us both a laughing stock.'

Ruby pulled a ridiculous face and found she was enjoying the unaccustomed role of clown. 'If you mind being laughed at, how are you going to feel when we're asked to sing and dance?'

'I can sing and dance,' said Slate, stiffly.

'So-rry,' replied Ruby before thinking she sounded just as mocking as Lee. 'I'm just impressed,' she added.

'No problem.' Slate looked so modest all of a sudden that Ruby thought he really must be good. 'Here,' he said, 'Take Aurora. I expect she'll sit on your arm.'

'Or my bucket,' suggested Ruby, unpacking her seaside bucket.

Slate eyed her critically. 'You look really stupid,' he said, 'but I like it.'

'Thanks.' Ruby had never believed it could feel good to be called stupid. 'Do you know it's actually stopped raining?' Moreover, the moon, directly overhead, had been joined by a mass of stars so that they were brilliantly lit. 'It's like being on the stage,' she murmured and saw that the light was strong enough to produce reflections on the windows of the hall, so that they shone brilliantly.

'Look at me!' cried Slate. Ruby had not seen the transformation but here, in front of her, stood a performer, sequinned cap, gleaming waistcoat and coiled up his arm and round his neck . . .

'Aaah!' shrieked Ruby. Abruptly, the snake slithered down and landed with a plop in the bucket that hung over Slate's arm.

'You frightened Cedric,' he said, reproachfully. 'He's very nervous of human beings. Why don't you give him a stroke?'

'No thank you,' shuddered Ruby. 'Anyway, he might eat Aurora.'

'He loves Aurora. Well, if he doesn't love her, he doesn't plan to eat her. You must be more trusting, Ruby.'

'Let's go in,' said Ruby hastily as Cedric's head rose tentatively above the rim of the bucket.

'Forward.' Slate took a purposeful step and Ruby suddenly became aware that fluttering above their heads, rising from a pole jutting above the door, was a flag on which she could make out the words, 'Audition for Life.'

CHAPTER FOUR

The Salvation Army Hall

The heavy door opened smoothly, no ghoulish creaks, no cobwebs to brush across your face and make you scream . . . Ruby was just thinking this when she felt herself knocked backwards not by a headless corpse but by an exuberance of warmth, light and noise. Forgetting Cedric, she grabbed Slate's arm.

'Darlings! Welcome to the auditions!' Someone or other with the voice she remembered from the answering machine message was standing in front of them. She was a little person with floating yellow hair but Ruby couldn't make out any more, or see what sort of room they were in because the warmth had completely misted over her glasses.

'I can't see a thing!' cried Ruby. And to make matters even more confusing, Aurora rose off her arm and fluttered round and round her head.

'Of course you can, darling!' The blurred figure in front of her (who Ruby remembered was called Cherie), leant forward and lifted off her glasses.

Usually, when Ruby took off her glasses, the world receded into a dull, grey fog; this time, exactly the opposite happened. Suddenly, everything was clear and bright. It was almost as if she had properly opened her eyes for the first time in her life. The hall, she saw, was crowded with children, many of them in some sort of school uniform, but all wearing a hat and carrying a bucket.

'Ruby. Ruby!' She realised Slate was pulling at her arm. 'This lot haven't brought real pet animals, they've brought stuffed ones!' He sounded aggrieved and accusing.

Ruby looked and saw the room was filled with animals, some clutched in their owner's arms, the larger ones (a hippopotamus and a crocodile for instance), on the floor, but none of them moving.

'Darlings!' Cherie was still standing in front of them, arm out-raised rather as if she might wave a wand (although now that Ruby looked at her more closely her hair was not blonde but white, which surely made her much too old to be a fairy). 'Darlings, these others are hopeless. You are far far better.

Come. April and Frederick are waiting for you.'

Slate looked at Ruby and Ruby looked at Slate. 'Where are your glasses?' asked Slate.

'I don't know,' said Ruby, quite truthfully because Cherie no longer held them, 'but it doesn't matter because I can see without them.' She paused before continuing with remarkable calmness. 'And one of the things I can see extremely clearly is that Cedric is out of your bucket and sliding off at quite a pace along the floor . . .'

She had hardly finished speaking and Slate had not time to dive at his pet's fast disappearing tail, before the general rather cheerful hubbub had abruptly changed into a rising shriek of terror in which the word 'Snake!' rose above everything.

In less than a minute, all the children, hats flying, buckets swinging, had charged past Ruby and Slate (who stood amazed) and dashed out into the dark world. As the hall became quiet, Ruby saw at the far end a man and a woman sitting chatting calmly. Cedric, she noticed, had reached them already and was neatly coiling himself on the space in front of them. Aurora, still attached by a string to Ruby's wrist, was trying to fly towards them, tugging so hard that she felt herself pulled forward.

Slate, about to make a dash to recapture Cedric, slowed down. Together, the two children walked forward.

'So you're the clever ones!' announced April Whipple. Slate and Ruby stared. She was a woman of startling beauty with shiny conker-coloured hair, wide green-blue eyes and a slim figure dressed in a silver tunic over tight black velvet trousers. Round her neck brilliant green stones glittered thrillingly.

'Oh, no,' said Ruby, very confused, not least because she had never been called clever before. 'We're not at all clever. We can't even sing and dance . . .'

'Oh, yes, we can,' interrupted Slate.

But before he could begin, Frederick Whipple had leant forward. 'Not necessary. Watch Cedric. Listen to Aurora.'

Frederick was as glamorous as April. He had black hair, blue eyes, wore a black silk shirt and bronze-coloured leather trousers. Ruby might have stared at him for some time, if Slate hadn't grabbed her arm.

'Hey, he's just never done that before.' Cedric was dancing. One half of his long body remained curled up while the rest swayed and shimmied, bowed and swooped and whirled. In awe, Ruby saw his magnificent head with its great raised ruff, his brilliant unblinking eyes, his darting tongue, black and forked.

'Man, I could never groove like that,' breathed Slate, admiringly. 'Cool, Cedric, cool.'

'He's dancing to Aurora's singing!' cried Ruby. 'I never knew doves sang like that.' Aurora's voice soared and trilled and rippled.

'It's like, it's like fabulous,' whispered Slate.

'Dear girl, why are you dripping? And why are you wearing such ridiculous and unflattering headgear?'

Sadly, Ruby realised the questions were addressed to her by the glorious April Whipple.

'It was raining,' she said dismally.

'But I can see your hair dripping.'

'That's because I only put the hat on when I arrived because I didn't want it to get wet.'

Ruby saw Frederick and April looking at each other. 'None of this matters, of course, my dear – although both you and Slate might have considered standing in your buckets, so much better for the floor. What matters is that you have both succeeded in the Audition for Life and you should now get the details for your journey to the Island from Cherie. Darling!' called April.

'The Island!' exclaimed Slate and Ruby in one voice. How they had succeeded in the audition they didn't care to enquire, but the idea of an island was as thrilling as it was extraordinary.

'Sssh,' said Cherie, appearing suddenly at their side. 'Now put Cedric in his bucket and Aurora in your hat and come with me.'

She led them away towards the door, and the very strange thing was that when Ruby looked over her shoulder, Frederick and April had completely disappeared.

'Now, you two,' said Cherie, who was beginning to seem rather bossy, 'Your tickets are here so all you have to do is turn up with small bags, packed with swimming gear, toiletries, light clothing including one sweater and wet weather gear. Time and place are on the tickets. Ruby, here are your spectacles. I'd give them a clean if I were you. Thank you.'

'But where is this island?' Slate tried to speak but somehow before he got an answer, they found themselves on the other side of the door to the hall, standing in the moonlight in gently falling rain. The hall itself was completely dark and, as they stared at it, seemed to become curiously more derelict.

'I'm sure there was a flag above the door,' faltered Ruby, hooking her glasses over her ears.

'And clock that ivy, like crawling in the windows,' added Slate, equally bemused.

'The roof!' exclaimed Ruby. 'There isn't a roof!'

'Weird, man!' In complete agreement, they both began to walk and then run away. Cedric slipped out of his bucket and Aurora untied her string and flew into the night. They ran as fast as they could through brambles and bushes and grasses until they burst through the blue door and arrived, scratched and panting, on the street. It seemed quite strange and, they had to admit it to themselves, reassuring, to see a large bus (advertising holiday islands as it happened) passing by.

'Quick!' shouted Slate. They swung on to the back of it and stood staring out at the wet pavements. Slate dropped his eyes to look at something in his hand. Ruby looked at the same thing in hers. Two slips of paper on which was written 'March 4th, 5 pm, Pier 147.'

'So it wasn't a dream. Wicked,' whispered Slate.

'Of course it wasn't a dream,' whispered Ruby, who was beginning to worry about arriving home later than her mother.

But Slate had another surprise. 'Hey, Ruby, look at my watch. What time does it say?'

Ruby looked. 'Five o'clock.' She did a double-take. 'But it must have been at least five o'clock when we found the hall.'

'Check.' Slate frowned in a bemused way.

'It must have stopped,' said Ruby before looking at her own watch and seeing that said five o'clock too.

'I'll tell you what,' Slate avoided Ruby's eyes as if embarrassed by what he was going to say, although he spoke with firm conviction. 'It's not our watches that stopped when we went into that hall, it's time!'

As they both looked at each other with excitement – now this really was an adventure unlike anything else – the bus conductor came shouting at them, 'Tickets, if you don't mind!'

Acting in unison again, they hastily stuffed the slips of paper into their pockets.

That night Ruby woke up abruptly. She had been dreaming, that's what it was. She sat up in the darkness and felt her heart pounding. She had been on this white beach, glaring white so that her eyes hurt and the waves were crashing down as hard and sharp as glass and then she had seen something coming out of the water towards her, black and horrible with teeth and a long, long body.

That was the moment she had woken up. It was more than an hour before Ruby fell asleep again.

CHAPTER FIVE

Bad bits at home

'Where did you go yesterday, then?' Lee attached herself to Ruby as soon as she arrived at school the next morning.

'What's it to you? I'm stu-pid, aren't I?' Ruby walked as fast as she could along the corridor but, given the relative length of their legs, there was no way she could shake Lee off. Running was strictly forbidden. So she stopped and confronted her. 'You wouldn't believe what happened even if I did tell you.'

'Try me.'

'No!'

'We're supposed to be best friends,' whined Lee.

Ruby looked at her shiny dark hair, heart-shaped face and long slim body. 'Well then, why are you always so nasty to me?' She had never felt so brave in her life as she left Lee standing and stalked into the classroom.

Unfortunately, as the day wore on she began to feel a great deal less brave. It was all very well having the prospect of a great adventure but not so good when your companion, that is Slate, never talks to you or even looks your way. As Ruby walked home by herself at the end of the day, she felt very pathetic indeed.

'Pier 147. Found out where it is, have you?' Slate caught up with her.

Ruby swung round on him crossly. 'No. And I don't see why I should talk to you when you don't talk to me all day.' She might have told him about her dream if he hadn't answered so quickly.

'I told you before. This is like about secrets, isn't it?' Slate stood swinging his bag, looking misunderstood. At that moment, Ruby caught sight of Lee walking purposefully towards them. 'Well, anyway,' she said, 'I might tell Lee about it.'

'But she didn't go for the audition! She's nothing to do with it.' Now Slate sounded really hurt. 'And if you'd cool it, I'll tell you what she's been saying about you.'

'I don't want to hear.' Ruby stuffed her fingers in her ears and began to walk briskly down the road. She thought all this was too much and all she wanted to do was to lie down on the sofa and watch television.

'Chill,' said Slate. 'Let's go back to my place. Aurora will calm you down.'

Ruby admitted to herself that even the thought of Aurora's cooing made her feel better. 'OK. Let's run then, before Lee catches up.'

As it turned out, Slate's home was anything but calming. Slate's brother, Brent, was there, ten years older, ten times bigger, ten times meaner.

'You think you're living in a pigsty, is that it?' he yelled at Slate as soon as they were in the house. 'Have you cleaned your room since you were born? And what do you think the kitchen is? Some kind of self-service cafeteria?'

Slate rolled his eyes at Ruby who was trying to keep her eyes down to avoid this onslaught. 'Chill, man,' he said, unwisely.

'Chill who?'

Slate bent double under a heavy cuff to his head. 'I'm going, I'm going,' he mumbled, slithering out of the room with Ruby shadowing him closely.

'And don't bring your stunted, fish-eyed friends here without asking!' Brent's voice followed them up the stairs.

Trying not to hear this insult, Ruby concentrated on Slate's room which, she had to admit, was the dirtiest and messiest she had ever seen. In fact, she couldn't find anywhere to sit down, not even the floor which was covered with clothes, CDs and several mugs partly filled with strange-coloured vegetation she preferred not to investigate further.

'Brent's not all bad,' said Slate, sweeping some stuff off his bed so that they could sit down. 'But he resents having a son to look after when he's not a father.'

'Oh,' Ruby thought how to put it delicately. 'Is your dad never around?'

'Check. You don't want to know about him. You don't want to know where my dad is and I don't want to tell you. Now about this Pier 147. Got your map have you?'

As a matter of fact Ruby did have her map. Together they spread it on the floor – at this point Ruby gave a shriek as she spotted Cedric curled up under the bed.

'Sssh, you'll wake him,' said Slate firmly.

So, together, they pored over the map. 'A pier usually is on the sea front,' suggested Ruby.

'But there isn't any sea here.' He paused. They looked at each other. 'There is, like, a river.'

'A very big river,' agreed Ruby, 'with boats and ships and . . .'

'Almost like a harbour,' added Slate.

'No, not like a harbour,' said Ruby, amazed at her bossiness. Perhaps once she escaped from Lee (and her mother, she thought to herself in brackets) she would turn out to be a very bossy person.

Either way, neither of them could find any reference to a pier.

'We've got three days,' said Slate, as Ruby folded the

map, saying it was time she got home or her mother would call the police.

'And I haven't even seen Aurora,' she realised disappointedly.

'Don't be silly. She's been here all the time. On that shelf above your head.'

Ruby looked up and saw the bird fast asleep, surrounded by rubbish. 'You should clean up,' she said irritably, standing and going to the door. 'There could be a dead body in here and you wouldn't know it.'

'You sound just like Brent. It's my room, isn't it?'

'There is something called "basic hygiene",' retaliated Ruby, quoting her mother, but this useful information was lost in the enthusiastic barking of four angry dogs, otherwise known as the Spice Girls, as Brent took them out their meal.

Ruby slid past them and dashed down the street. She was going to be late.

'You're late.' Ruby's mother held open the door with one hand while holding a glass in the other. This was a bad sign. Ruby knew that an early gin and bitter lemon meant that her mother was tired, cross and wondering why she struggled on. 'I don't know why I struggle on,' she said now. 'Nobody cares.'

'Sorry, Mum.' Ruby came in and put down her bag. She did feel sorry for Mrs Gutch who worked as much as six days a week to keep them in funds, even if most days she actually enjoyed her job. 'Hairdressing is more than a job, it's a vocation,' she liked to boast on good days. Sometimes she added, 'If you knew the stories my clients tell me, you'd think I was priest, best friend and psychiatrist rolled into one.' On good days her dyed blonde hair was puffed up in fountains all over her head and her eyes gleamed blue and round. On bad days, the fountain dribbled round her head and her eyes were full and inward looking. 'Sorry I'm late, Mum. Were you worried?'

'Of course I wasn't worried. I knew you'd be with that Lee with the *two* parents.'

'She can't help having two parents,' said Ruby, deciding it was hardly a lie not to contradict her mother. If she had seen Slate's home, she'd have put him right out of bounds. Suddenly she found herself overtaken by a long shiver. Could she really be planning to go to an unknown island with a boy older than her who lived with troupes of wild animals and no parents?'

'Go and give yourself a good wash,' Mrs Gutch sniffed disapprovingly. 'I'm sure you smell of animal.'

'Oh no!' exclaimed Ruby, which really was a lie.

Despite all her anxieties, over a tea of scrambled eggs on toast, Ruby found herself asking intently, 'Mum, do you know where Pier 147 is?'

'What kind of question is that?' Mrs Gutch looked over the rim of her glass which contained her second gin and bitter lemon. On her bad days, she thought she was fat and did not eat, although Ruby had once looked up gin in her mother's calorie control book and found two glasses of gin and bitter lemon scored higher than a bar of chocolate.

'It's for school,' explained Ruby, guiltily clocking up another lie.

'I don't know about number 147, but it's not a nice place to go to, not at all . . .'

'Oh, we're not going there,' interrupted Ruby, finding lies tripping off her tongue.

'I once went there for an outing on a boat. Before your dad took off. A dark threatening place, old warehouses, drugs, guns, big dogs, people you don't want to know about . . . worse than where that Salvation Army hall was you were asking about the other day. . .'

'But where is it?'

'At the end of the number 225 bus route. Your dad and I had such a row I swore never to speak to him again. There was a storm too, lightning, thunder, the boat had covering, of course, but it leaked, and there were waves enough to make you think you were at sea not on some mucky great river . . . Leastways I was sea-sick and if you think your dad cared . . .'

'I've finished, Mum.' Ruby pushed away her plate and got up to go to her room. The other thing about Mrs Gutch's bad days was that she talked a lot about the past, always telling the bad bits. Or perhaps there were only bad bits.

That night Ruby didn't have a bad dream but she lay awake just the same, thinking. And what she was thinking was, that she had had just about enough of her mother's bad days and bad bits, and that she didn't think it was fair she was blamed for her dad running off. She hadn't asked to be born early and so tiny. If anything, it was her mother's fault for smoking so much when she was pregnant. Which added up to the fact that what she, Ruby, needed was an adventure all of her own which would show her mother she could manage perfectly well on her own. At this point, Ruby began to feel too sleepy for any more thinking. However she whispered, 'Pier 147' into the darkness as a kind of promise to herself.

CHAPTER SIX

Waking up to it

'I know where we have to go!' The following morning Ruby grabbed Slate's arm, having noticed that, for once, he wasn't surrounded by his gang.

'Like where?' asked Slate out of the side of his mouth as if he didn't really care. At least he was admitting she existed.

'My mum told me. She says it's a horrible place . . .' As Ruby began to explain she saw, to her dismay, that Lee was coming down the corridor. Slate spotted her at the same time.

'I'm off. Is that girl your shadow or something?'

'Wait,' pleaded Ruby. But Slate had sloped off, passing

Lee with eyes half shut and a curl to his mouth. Ruby waited resignedly for Lee.

'I saw you run away from me last night,' she began at once. She jerked her head at Slate's fast disappearing back.

'We've got things to talk about.'

'Please, Ruby, you might at least listen.'

'Listen to what?'

'Listen to me saying sorry.' Ruby, who had started to walk away, stopped dead and stared at her once best friend with amazement. 'Yeah, I've been missing you these last few days and it made me think. And what I thought was, you're more fun to be with than anyone else, even if you are more or less a dwarf with the worst case of fuzzy orange hair I've ever seen.'

'Lee!'

'Well, you wouldn't want me to tell a lie, would you?'

'Yes, I would!' Once again Ruby walked away, but Lee still wasn't going to give up.

'I came to invite you to come over and stay the night. Mum and Dad are both out and they've got that sitter who only speaks some funny language. Mum's buying chicken kievs and chocolate milkshakes and leaving us a surprise video. Go on, Ruby. It's Dad's work dance. They won't be back till after midnight.'

'OK,' said Ruby, thinking invitations like this didn't come her way every day.

* * *

Ruby couldn't help comparing Lee's house with Slate's. For one thing it was in a street where every house was neatly kept with a little garden behind and a little garden in front with a neatly clipped hedge.

Inside, it was even grander, with everything clean and matching. For example, thought Ruby looking round the living room, the cushions not only matched each other but they matched the curtains too. Her own mother would have loved that, but she was too tired after working all day, whereas Lee's mother didn't have a job. 'I've got quite enough on my hands with Bob [who was her husband] and Lee,' Ruby had once overheard her say on the telephone.

What that meant, as far as Ruby could see, was that she never left either of them alone from the moment they walked through the door. Perhaps that explained Lee's mixture of spoilt and needy.

At this moment Lee was raiding the fridge. Mouth full of ice cream, she smiled at Ruby, 'I can only have a good time when *she's* out.' And Ruby had no need to ask who 'she' was. 'Let's dress up,' suggested Lee, abandoning the fridge and dashing for the stairs, 'before that babysitter woman comes.'

Ruby followed less enthusiastically. They'd dressed up once before when Lee's mother was out. Basically, it involved first sitting at her frilled dressing-table and trying out all her neatly arranged make-up and then moving on to the wardrobe where she kept a whole row of evening dresses.

'She only wears them once. It's a waste. If we didn't try them on, they'd hang here year in year out.' Lee tugged down a blue sequinned number with a swirly chiffon underskirt and began to rip off her school uniform.

It wasn't that Ruby wouldn't have enjoyed doing the same but, even though many of the labels said 'petite' which she knew meant small, they were at least a foot too long. 'I'll sit on the bed and watch you,' she said. So Lee pranced and twirled while she acted an enthralled audience – which was exactly what had happened last time.

She could have used the make-up, of course, but when she took off her glasses she couldn't see her face very clearly, so the result last time she tried had been extremely strange. And anyway none of the bright-coloured lipsticks and eye-shadows seemed quite right with her orange hair and freckles.

It was a relief when Lee suddenly noticed the time on her mother's gilded clock and shrieked, 'We've got to tidy up now!' She panicked further, 'Ludmilla will be here any minute!'

Ruby sighed. This had happened last time too. Lee had insisted everything must be left spotless. It had taken ages. She thought of Slate's disgusting bedroom and smiled to herself. There had to be a happy medium. At least they were one step nearer the chicken kievs; admiring Lee definitely had its limits. Tomorrow, she thought, feeling more cheerful, she'd tell Slate about the number 225 bus.

School assembly was taking longer than usual. The headmaster was giving a lecture about children who were refugees. Ruby had never thought about refugees before. In the school there were all kinds of different looking children, some with dark skins, some with light, some speaking English just like she did, some with accents that marked them out as not having grown up in England. And that was nothing to do with the colour of their skins. But she'd never really thought about how they came to live in her city. They were just part of her life, nice children, nasty children. But that wasn't what the headmaster was talking about, he was talking about refugees.

'There are some people,' he was saying, 'who are not safe in their own country and come here to our country as refugees.'

So that was it. Refugees had fled danger in their own homes and found new ones in England.

'I'm hoping,' continued the headmaster, 'that we'll be lucky enough to have a few of these unfortunate children come to our school and I want you to make them especially welcome. It won't be easy for them, learning a new language, finding new friends . . .'

When he had finished, Ruby, fired with enthusiasm clapped as loud as she could and for at least an hour afterwards forgot to think about the *Audition for Life*. Then she saw Slate.

'So, are you going to be especially welcoming?' He put

his hands together, raised his eyes imploringly.

'Don't make fun.' Ruby was truly shocked.

'You don't think like I'm a poor, sad refugee?'

'Of course I don't. No more than me or Lee.'

Slate abruptly resumed his usual arrogant slouch. 'Just joking!'

'Do you want to know where this pier is? Or shall we call it a day?' Ruby felt she was perfectly justified in showing a bit of adult weariness herself.

'Sure I do.'

'Well, we take the 225 bus. It goes all the way.' Ruby paused. 'On the other hand, I'm not sure I'm coming with you.' Ruby had no idea why she came out with this the day after she'd decided the thing she most needed was to escape her mother. But if she was trying to get a reaction from Slate, she certainly succeeded.

'You what?' Never too good with words, Slate seemed silenced by her remark. But his face showed such disappointment that Ruby turned her head away. He even looked as if he might start crying.

'I just said, I'm not sure. That's all.'

'What's all is you're a coward.' He turned his back sharply and seemed about to go.

Ruby grabbed his arm. 'It's not that.'

'What is it then?'

'Well, you can't just walk away. From home . . .'

'Huh!' snorted Slate, and Ruby saw that maybe his home might be quite easy to walk away from.

'From school, from friends . . .' Ruby stopped as he

gave another snort. 'You always seem at the centre of the cool crowd . . .'

'Huh!'

'I do wish you'd stop snorting.'

'You're just a coward. And I thought you were my friend and understood things.' Slate began to talk very quickly, slurring his words together so Ruby could hardly understand him. 'You were just messing me about. Like everybody else. Coming to the audition. I don't know why. Thinking you're better than me. I bet you didn't even see the card . . .'

'I did! I did!' Now it was Ruby's turn to interrupt.

'Then you *are* a rotten coward. And I wish I'd never known you!' Again he started walking away, adding over his shoulder with a not very convincing defiance, 'I expect I'll go alone.'

Ruby hesitated. She was pretty certain she was a coward. When she was with Lee, Lee took all the decisions. But it had been different with Slate. She had felt brave with him. Somehow life had seemed brighter, more risky certainly, but much more exciting. Did she want to throw all that up and go back to the old way?

'Slate,' Ruby called, 'I only said I wasn't absolutely sure I was coming with you. Of course, I am really. I've got to get out of my home for a bit.'

Slate came to her at once and, standing close, spoke intensely. 'You, like sometimes, you have to take risks. The right sort of risks, that is, otherwise you get nowhere.'

45

'That's just what I was thinking,' said Ruby stoutly, although her heart had started its dreadful pounding. 'Sometimes you just have to head into the unknown and forget what you're leaving behind.

'To the Island!' shouted Slate, dark eyes gleaming.

CHAPTER SEVEN

The Journey

It was already dark on the afternoon that Ruby and Slate set off for the 225 bus stop. Slate's backpack was so big that it seemed likely to pull him over backwards.

'What've you got there?' asked Ruby.

'Nothing special,' Slate answered, without meeting her eyes. He was hunched forward so far he looked like a tortoise under a shell.

It had been dark all day. At lunchtime, there had been a huge storm and several slates from the school roof had flung themselves to the ground, cutting a boy in the playground, who had to be taken to hospital. Even then, the clouds didn't clear away, swirling heavily about the sky and every now and again tipping out bursts of rain, even sleet on one occasion.

Ruby shivered, 'I don't know why we have to take such a long way round to the bus stop.'

'You want people to ask questions?'

'You're right. I'm sorry.' Ruby looked over her shoulder. In fact she had a funny feeling that they were being followed. As she'd turned her head she was just aware of a shadow disappearing behind a wall, but maybe it was only her imagination. Slate was even more tense than usual and she didn't want him to think she was losing her nerve again. However when they reached the stop she couldn't resist airing one of her continuing worries, 'How long do you think we'll be gone?'

Slate set the huge backpack carefully on the pavement before answering. There was no one else waiting for a bus and he seemed more relaxed. 'Brent won't miss me, if that's what you mean. Nor will I miss him. If he doesn't cool it when I get back I shall leave like forever.'

This was too scary an idea to tackle in their present situation so Ruby decided to change the subject. 'Do you think there could be an island in a river?' she asked.

'Not the sort of island where you'd need swimming gear. Not the sort of wicked faraway island we're going to.' They were standing in front of two tower apartment blocks which, like all tower blocks, were causing the wind to whip round them even more furiously. An old plastic bag caught round Slate's legs and he kicked it away. 'To tell you the truth,' said Slate, 'I've had enough of this city.'

'But we're not exactly running away!' Ruby thought of her mother and, although she wouldn't have chosen her if there was a choice in such things, she didn't wish to make her unhappy – or at least more unhappy than she was on her bad days.

'Speak for yourself.' Slate opened a flap on his backpack and took out a stick of chewing gum. He didn't offer Ruby any.

Ruby thought that if she were running away (which she wasn't, she was merely taking a brave step into the unknown), she wouldn't run away with someone as antisocial as Slate. His cool manner began to feel more like common rudeness. Over her shoulder she caught a glimpse of that shadow again.

'Here's the bus!' shouted Slate, his whole manner changing from slouch to wild enthusiasm. As they hauled their packs inside the bus Ruby wondered whether part of Slate's problem was the same sort of nervousness she felt.

The bus was altogether empty upstairs. Slate and Ruby sat at the very front, so far forward there was nothing but the dark night, filled once more with thunder and lightning, ahead of them. Once they had passed through the forest of tower blocks, there were far fewer buildings or at least there were no lights visible, as if those buildings they could see were uninhabited.

'I've never been this way before,' said Slate.

'Nor me,' shuddered Ruby as a roll of thunder sounded above the noise of the bus's engine. 'Did you remember your ticket for the Island?'

'Sure.' He paused, 'Hey, man, are you like as scared as me?'

'Scared rigid!' Both of them began to giggle hysterically and suddenly they were friends again.

'What I meant to say when you were asking about how long we'd be away and running away and all that,' Slate pushed up the long sleeve of his anorak, 'is that I've been checking my watch. You know what happened at that Salvation Army place. Well, the moment we stepped on this bus, my watch stopped. Look for yourself.'

Ruby looked and then checked her own watch. Both had stopped at exactly the same time. 'So my mother won't be worried.'

' 'Course not.'

'Oh,' sighed Ruby, trying unsuccessfully to hide her relief.

'I think,' said Slate slowly, 'Like we're going into a different space, like where real life rules don't apply, about not speaking to strangers and things.'

'You mean we're in a different world?'

'Like a different world,' repeated Slate. 'That's what Audition for Life is about. That's what I think.'

'That's what I think too,' said Ruby, a bit surprised that it was Slate and not her who'd found the words for what she'd been starting to realise herself. 'We can just be ourselves, doing whatever we choose to do.'

'Right on.'

One of the strange things about the bus journey was that for a good ten minutes the bus never stopped at all. When Ruby pointed this out, Slate looked thoughtful. 'I guess if there's no one getting in and no one getting out, there's no point in stopping.' After a pause, he added, 'But it'll have to stop at the end.'

'Wherever that is.'

'Chill,' advised Slate, smiling. And at that moment the bus stopped with a sharp jerk. From below, the driver's voice bellowed up to them, 'All change! All out!'

Hastily, Ruby and Slate dashed back down the bus and down the stairs. The driver was just a black silhouette in his cab. As they hauled their bags out of the door, he started the engine again, and, as soon as they were out, standing in the night, buffeted by wind and rain, he was turning the bus and heading back on the road they came, so fast that very soon, even the winking red tail-lights had disappeared. Ruby and Slate stared until Ruby's glasses were splodged with rain.

'I know just what refugees feel like,' she said, 'not knowing where they are and everything. Do you remember what Mr Harpsden said in assembly? About them having no proper home and not being able to speak the language. Being in an unknown country.'

'We've only come on an hour's bus ride from our homes. And as far as I know, if anyone was around, they'd speak the same language as us.'

'I still feel like one. Where are we anyway?'

They both took a step or two forward. It really was very dark. The lightning had passed and thick clouds hid the moon and stars.

'I think there's a wall or something ahead.'

Holding out their hands in front of them as if they were blind, they took a few more cautious steps.

'What's that noise?' asked Ruby.

'It might be water.'

'The river!'

They reached the wall, which turned out to be a low parapet, at the same moment as the wind blew one cloud so hard that the one behind it couldn't catch up, and the moon got a chance to beam through the gap.

'It is the river,' whispered Slate. (They were both whispering for some reason.) 'And to our right, there's some steps and I think there's a sign saying Pier 147.'

'What's that sliding down the steps?' cried Ruby, just before the gap closed and darkness came again.

'Probably a cat.' And on cue they both heard a loud meowing. Ruby, however, remained convinced that she had caught sight of some thing or person much larger than a cat.

'We'd better get our bags.' Neither of them admitted it, but what they'd really have liked to see by the moonlight, was a nice, friendly, well-lit boat, steaming along the river to pick them up. Perhaps playing jolly music and serving delicious food and drinks.

Cold and wet, hungry and tired, they dragged their

packs to the top of the steps and, feeling rather sorry for themselves (and a bit silly too – maybe it was all a practical joke), they settled down to wait.

The boat rushed out of the darkness. It was small and black with one hard beam of light.

'Slate! Oh look!' shouted Ruby. They grabbed their bags as the boat executed a sharp turn, sweeping water over the lower steps and came to rest quietly. A figure stood up at the wheel. 'Audition for Life!' His voice sounded slightly foreign. He had turned the light off so they could see no more than a black silhouette.

'Coming!' shouted Slate. Again he was heaving his bag.

'Slate!' called Ruby, following as close as she could, 'what's that hissing coming from your bag?'

'Cedric,' answered Slate briefly.

'I can't believe it! You've brought a huge snake . . .' Ruby would have continued but just at the bottom of the steps, where the water was sloshing around and the boat banged, there seemed to be a third dark figure – but perhaps she was muddled. At any rate she was more worried about getting into the boat which was bobbing all over the place. Eventually a strong arm pulled her in and she fell with her pack into the bottom of the boat. Just as she was struggling to get up the engine roared and she fell back down again as the boat took off at such a tremendous speed that the bow was tipped up out of the water and the stern slid down at a steep angle.

'Oh, oh, oh,' a voice beside her whimpered.

'Who's a coward now, Slate?' But this wasn't Slate. Slate was standing at the front of the boat with the captain. She could see his silhouette.

'I'm not Slate.' It was a very frightened girl's voice, which now was half smothered by tears. 'I didn't want you to have all the fun. I've been following you. And then I didn't want to be left in that horrid place.' The tears now completely overwhelmed the words.

'Lee! You're . . . you're . . .' For a moment Ruby was lost for words. 'You're a stowaway!'

'I know.' A very small voice. 'I'm sorry.' More tears.

'But you can't come! You didn't believe in the weird card on the notice board. You never came to the audition. This isn't your adventure!' Ruby was furious. She pushed and shoved Lee so that the boat began to rock.

'Keep still back there!' The captain half-turned and shouted.

Slate turned right round. 'Isn't this great? Whatever's the matter with you?'

Lee pulled at Ruby's arm. 'Don't tell him I'm here,' she pleaded.

'He'll find out,' hissed Ruby. But Slate had turned back again and was watching the light beam cutting a sharp path through the water. Ruby lay back, too tired to make any decisions. However, as Lee relaxed backwards too, she couldn't resist one jibe. 'Careful Lee, there's a snake in that bag!' It was too dark to see Lee's face but the quickly suppressed shriek of horror caused Ruby to smile contentedly to herself. Maybe it wouldn't be too bad to have Lee tag along on condition she, Ruby, kept the upper hand.

So the small boat sped across the water, the bright light in front, the white wake behind and, on either side, tall buildings, some as dark as the sky, others blazing with light where dark figures moved as if on a stage. Now and again the buildings parted and there was a blank as if leading to an uninhabited space. It was at one of these break points that the boat swivelled left abruptly causing Lee and Ruby to tumble together. When they unscrambled from each other, they realised the boat had changed course entirely and was heading down a narrow inlet with flat plains on either side.

'Wherever we're going we must be nearly there,' whispered Ruby. 'You'd better get ready to run.'

'We're in the middle of *nowhere*,' Lee whispered back. 'Where would I run to?'

Once again Slate turned round, 'I can see lights ahead,' he shouted excitedly, 'red and green, a string of white . . . I think it's an airport.'

At that moment a rumbling which they had become vaguely aware of, turned into a vast noise filling up all the space above their heads. It was a helicopter, its huge belly passing directly over them, its gigantic propellers beating the air. The boat began to jump and skid, as waves, churned up by the wind in the helicopter's path, lashed at its sides.

'Hold tight!' commanded their captain. He was slowing down and now, instead of banging into the waves, they began to rise with the crests and sink into the troughs.

'I feel like a duck,' whispered Ruby, before thinking she wanted to be at the front of the boat with Slate. She scrambled forward. Slate helped her to squeeze in beside him.

'It's a heliport,' he said. 'This must be the next stage of our journey.' Ruby wondered whether to tell him about Lee but, glimpsing the captain's stern profile decided she couldn't risk her being pushed overboard, even if she was only her ex-best friend.

They were approaching a jetty now, unlit except for their own beam, but by this she could make out another man waiting to receive them. At least she supposed it was a man, although a very, very small man.

'Darlings, welcome!' It was Cherie, the little woman with the white-blonde hair, expertly catching the rope thrown by the captain, bustling and hustling them off the boat, loading their packs on to a trolley. 'Hurry, hurry! The rest of us have been waiting for ages.'

The boat had already set off again, taking its light with it and they were crossing a dim strip of concrete, before Ruby thought to look for Lee. Somehow she must have got off in the bustle – unless she was being carried back down river again.

'Who are the rest of us?' panted Slate. Cherie was actually running with the trolley now.

'Other children, do you think?' They could see where they were aiming now; a helicopter standing in readiness about fifty yards away. As they neared it, the propellers began to turn.

'Duck your heads!' instructed Cherie.

The wind blew so fiercely that Ruby's face was half smothered by her wild hair. The noise was so painfully loud that she stuffed her fingers in her ears and, like this, mostly blind, mostly deaf, climbed up into the helicopter. She was met by a suffocating wave of warmth and light and the sound of children's voices, all apparently shouting as loud as they could. Pushing her hair out of her eyes, she saw that the reason was quite straightforward; they were all wearing heavy sound mufflers over their ears.

'Sit here, darlings.' Cherie indicated a very small space. Ruby squeezed in beside Slate obediently, but she was beginning to think she might rebel against all these orders if some one didn't offer some explanations soon. 'Put these over your ears, darlings,' commanded Cherie. The truth was, even if she did ask questions, no one would hear them.

'They've put Cedric in the hold,' Slate grabbed her arm and mouthed into her face so she could understand him. Ruby suddenly wondered if perhaps Lee was there too but she couldn't take any of this very seriously, because she could feel the helicopter rising and then they were in the air. Looking around, she saw that everyone had stopped talking as if this sensation of being airborne should be appreciated in silence. Ruby counted six other children, all about the same age. Tall, short, fat, thin, dark, fair, all sorts. Three wearing school uniform, three in jeans and jackets like they were. Three girls, three boys. They must have passed the audition too, she thought. She nudged Slate and mouthed, 'Where do you think we're going?'

As she spoke, she felt a nudge on her right and a small boy, large eyes filled with excitement, mouthed back at her, 'The Island!' He wore school uniform, old-fashioned grey shorts, long socks and a blazer with red stripe.

'What's your name? she mouthed.

'St Ives.'

'I thought that was a place.'

'Mais oui. It is too.' He was the youngest there, Ruby thought, and wondered why he spoke partly in French. She tugged at Slate, 'This is St Ives.' But Slate was craning to see out of the small window behind them.

'We're coming down!' he yelled so loudly that Ruby and St Ives could hear him quite clearly. 'It looks like a proper airport below.'

CHAPTER EIGHT

Onward to the Island

The helicopter dropped quite quickly, leaving their stomachs several hundred yards above them. The moment they touched ground, Cherie grabbed Slate and Ruby and announced they were her helpers. Together they collected the ear mufflers. Again everything was speed and hurry.

'Out! Out! Darlings! We don't want to miss the next stage, do we?'

Ruby whispered to Slate, 'It's like being in a computer game.'

'Like I was thinking the same. Super cool.' Slate was clearly having the best time.

A small hand took Ruby's, 'What is a computer game?' Slate and Ruby looked at St Ives full of amazement. Where had he sprung from? Not knowing what a computer game was! But there was no time to answer him because they were being rushed out of the back of the helicopter, down the steps and on to the tarmac.

'This way,' called Cherie.

Up until this point, although rushed and strange, everything had been smoothly organised, even in the darkness, everything was calm. But now there was sudden chaos. The baggage had just been lifted out and with it had come a slim figure, yowling and crying.

'Lee!' squeaked Ruby.

'I opened this bag,' sobbed Lee, 'and a huge snake came out.' Cherie bent over her, tut-tutting, and wiping her face with a red and white spotted handkerchief.

'Cedric!' shouted Slate, chasing across the tarmac. Two or three other boys followed, whooping loudly.

'Oh dear,' Cherie looked up from mopping up Lee, 'Frederick and April won't be pleased if we're late.' She turned back to Lee. 'Who are you, darling? It can't have been very comfortable in with the baggage.'

'I'm Ruby's best friend, Lee,' the sobbing stopped abruptly. 'At least I was until she met Slate.'

'Well, you're quite a brave young girl. Now how are we going to get you home again?'

'No! No!' wailed Lee, not being brave at all, Ruby thought. 'I want to come with you! Please don't send me back. I won't be a nuisance, I promise.'

As they were speaking, Slate, St Ives and the other excited boys returned with Cedric slung round Slate's neck.

'We seem to have not one but two stowaways,' commented Cherie, showing as much indulgence to the snake as she had to Lee.

'There you are, my darling.' She tickled Cedric under the neck and he yawned delightedly.

'Actually there're three stowaways.' Slate yanked at his bag and Aurora flew out of it.

Cherie laughed merrily, 'Five for the price of two.'

Ruby was about to say she had nothing to do with Lee's arrival and to point out Lee hadn't passed the audition when, even in the darkness, she saw the desperation on her face. After all, it wasn't for her to make the decision. Meanwhile, Cherie was calmly leading them across the runway towards an aeroplane whose engines were already running. It seemed they were off again, Lee, Cedric and Aurora included.

The aeroplane was not very big. Ruby, sitting with Slate near the back, counted twenty children including themselves. After they had taken off, it was quiet enough to hear everyone asking the same question. 'Where are we going?' 'Where are we going?' 'Do *you* know where we are going?' But nobody came up with an answer. They only knew what they had known at the beginning: they were going to an island, but the island could be anywhere in the world. There was nothing else for it but to settle down comfortably, eat the food provided on individual trays and enjoy the journey.

After an hour or two, those who hadn't brought headphones or something to read fell asleep. Looking at her watch automatically, Ruby remembered it had stopped.

'Anyone know what time it is?' Lee looked at her watch obligingly but it had stopped too.

'C'est minuit, I think,' piped up St Ives who was sitting next to Lee across the aisle, and they all agreed he was probably right. At least, midnight seemed as good as any other time.

St Ives piped up again, this time, thankfully, in English, although with rather a strong French accent. 'Nobody cares where I am since the death of Poppy and Hubert.'

'What weird names!' commented Slate.

'Mes parents.' St Ives voice was dignified. 'We lived in France in a caravan à côté d'une plage. A beach, as you say. Alors, they have died in a car crash and my grand-mère make me go to boarding school in Devon. A horrible school.' Here St Ives shuddered theatrically. 'It is on a cliff with big wind and cold sea. J'adore the sea but not cold booming at night. At night I cry. Everybody hate me because I speak French, even the teachers. I must stay there in the holy holidays, except when my grand-mère takes me. She lives dans une maison énorme, with a cook and des domestiques. Every day she calls me a cruel mistake. She hates mon père for being French and making ma mère live in a caravan in ugly France so she hates me too. I am a tragedy. And France is not ugly. C'est le pays le plus beau du monde.'

St Ives told this sad story with such gusto that neither Ruby nor Slate knew quite what to say. The funny mix of French and English made it all seem odder, although they managed to pick up most of the words. Eventually, Ruby decided he didn't want sympathy. 'I think it's cool to speak French,' she said.

'Like maybe it'll come in useful where we're going,' suggested Slate.

They all thought about this.

'I know where we're going,' said Lee. She was speaking across St Ives. The three others looked at her in surprise, not just because of what she'd just said but because this was the first time she had spoken since they'd got on to the plane, as if she were afraid of being thrown off it if she drew attention to herself. Actually, they were sort of taking no notice of her too because she hadn't won the right to be with them.

'It was when I was in that dreadful hold with the baggage,' she shuddered. 'There was a bag by me, not Slate's.' She looked nervously upward where Cedric curled on the shelf. 'It was very colourful, all stripes and spots and swirls. It had a label but nothing was written on it; there was just a picture. I didn't notice it at first but then I couldn't help but look because it gave out light – in fact it was like a mini screen, moving images, the sea, palm trees, people in the distance, small white clouds moving across a blue sky. That's where we must be going. It was so beautiful.'

Ruby looked at Lee sternly. 'You weren't dreaming?'

Lee gave her a half-smile. 'You weren't dreaming when you saw the card in school about the Audition for Life. I know that now. And I'm sorry I made fun.'

Ruby and Slate looked at each other. 'It was probably Cherie's bag you saw,' said Slate. And somehow Lee seeing Cherie's bag and the label made her seem one of them. In a way, her chase after them, all on her own, at night, was like a different sort of audition, perhaps as hard as theirs. Ruby smiled at her for the first time.

'I think you were very brave getting into that hold.'

'I saw une carte aussi,' St Ives had been trying to speak for some time. 'Toutes les couleurs. On the wall in my horrible school. I know it is for me. Audition for Life. I can escape.'

'So you like auditioned, did you?' For once Slate seemed interested in someone else's adventures.

'Mais oui. I must go to the plage, the beach, with a hat, a bucket and a pet.'

Ruby began to laugh. 'Do you think all over England, kids were going off like that?'

'All the kids in this plane. Unreal, man.' Slate flapped his hand at the seats in front.

'So what happened when you saw the card?' Lee asked St Ives earnestly, while Ruby noted how surprisingly nice Lee was being to this funny little half-French boy.

'I told two of the other boys who told me I show off

64

and needed a peg taking down. So they take off mon pantalon and throw me in a nettlebed.' Here St Ives rubbed his bare leg vigorously.

'What's this pantalon?' asked Slate.

'Trousers,' said Lee, 'and then?'

'Alors I telephone le numéro and voilà la belle ange Cherie tell me I have passed the audition and a boat will be waiting on the beach. We go across the sea. La belle mer. C'est ça. Je suis here.'

'With friends!' exclaimed Lee.

'With friends,' agreed Ruby, looking hopefully at the other children, some of whom had shut their eyes and seemed settled in for a sleep.

'It's all French to me,' grumbled Slate, rubbing his eyes and yawning.

The truth was that, after so many adventures, they were all feeling worn out and somehow the not knowing where they were going – even though Lee's tropical island sounded exciting – made them feel even more tired.

In the end none of the children knew how far they'd flown. Night came with them all the way and all of them slept at some time or another. They woke to darkness still with the sound of the engine noise changing and Aurora cooing gently.

'I guess we're coming down!' Everybody, even the sleepiest, crowded at the windows trying to see out. But there was nothing to see, only more and more blackness until, at last, Slate spotted two rows of lights.

'This is the longest night I've ever known,' sighed Ruby, as the aeroplane hit the runway and once more Cherie was chivvying them outside. But this time, there was something very different about the experience.

'It's so warm,' whispered Lee. 'The air's as soft as velvet.'

'I can smell the sea!'

Behind them the row of lights lit up tall trees like upside down floor mops. 'Palm trees!' exclaimed Slate. It seemed that Lee's island image might be right.

'Now, now darlings. Time to stretch your legs. Raymond will bring your bags.' Cherie lined them up and gave one out of two a torch. 'Just follow me, through the palm grove and out to the jetty.' So they were not yet out to sea but heading that way. 'Hurry, hurry.' Cherie gave them no more time to think and only just time to notice a large man with a buggy. Presumably this was Raymond.

Stumbling and holding on to each other, they filed into the darkness, entering into the great trunked palms nervously but at the same time aware that the smell of the sea had become stronger. Soon they could hear a booming noise.

'Les grosses vagues,' exclaimed St Ives, in a pleased-sounding voice. 'Big warm waves. Like French waves.'

'I've only been to the sea once,' Ruby whispered to Slate, 'and there were no waves to make a noise like that.'

'I've never seen the sea except on TV,' admitted Slate.

Now they were out beyond the trees and a vast

expanse of water took up all the space that wasn't sky. It was still dark but they could see the edge of it by the white curl of the waves as they crashed on the sand. Soon they were blundering along beside a beach, sand and shells and sharp pebbles, kicking round their ankles. Somewhere, someone seemed to be whimpering, almost crying. Ruby tried to identify where the sound came from – a tallish figure behind her, she thought.

She dropped back, 'Are you all right?' The girl, at least it was probably a girl, did not answer at once but eventually produced a spattering of incomprehensible words. 'You're foreign, aren't you?' A few more meaningless words stuttered out. 'I'm sorry. I can't understand.' There was only one thing to do. Ruby took her/his hand firmly and was immediately tightly gripped.

'Nadire,' the girl said.

'Ruby,' replied Ruby, trying to sound as calm and comforting as possible.

Everybody was so taken up with picking their way through the darkness that no one noticed Ruby had a new companion. It was extraordinary to sense a great ocean ahead of them without being able to see it. But, at last (although none of them dared mention it in case it was their imagination), they saw a slight lightening where the water might make a horizon with the sky. Perhaps the sun would rise after what had seemed like at least three night-times worth of darkness.

'Darlings, you are slower than tortoises!' called Cherie. And there was a jetty and bobbing alongside it a white painted launch. They could see that easily enough, with lights strung along the deck and Raymond already loading in their baggage and two or three other crew. And wasn't that Cedric coiled around the railings, just above where 'Audition for Life' was painted in bold colours that seemed to change from red to purple to blue to green to orange to yellow and back again? They piled on, suddenly wide awake and chattering and laughing. All except Nadire who was silently gripping Ruby's hand so hard it hurt.

'Look, there's Aurora,' Ruby retrieved her hand with some relief and pointed upwards so Nadire too could see the pigeon fluttering above a flag flying at the front of the ship.

They went follow-my-leader into the ship which plunged restively in the waves and, as soon as the last of them were in, the ropes were untied and they were speeding to an uncertain destination.

The bright gap widened between the water and the sky. It was the sky, Ruby knew, but they had been so long in the dark that this slice of ever-increasing brilliance seemed like another world. The boat was going very fast. At the stern it left a huge trail of white churned-up water, and at the bow it dug deeply into the dark waves, throwing up white spume on either side.

Ruby, Nadire, Slate, St Ives and Lee stood at the front, hanging on to the railings. Their hair strung out behind them, wet and tangled. Their faces were salty wet too, their clothes flattened against their bodies. They all looked forward, staring at the brightening light. It had changed from a misty grey to a lemon yellow and now it was becoming harder and sharper. It was at the exact moment that the sun, a great red fiery ball, rose from behind the water and took over the sky, that they first saw the island. It was a slim black silhouette against the burning, red and orange-yellow.

They had been silent before but now they could no longer contain themselves.

'The Island!' they all shrieked in different accents and even different languages.

CHAPTER NINE

Towards the Sun

Once they had spotted the island, it became bigger and closer remarkably quickly. The sun rose fast too, much faster, they all felt, than in England and, despite the wind from the speeding boat, they were beginning to feel a powerful heat.

Standing beside Ruby, Nadire made some kind of remark in her difficult language and huddled even closer. Irritated, Ruby moved away and turned to look at her properly for the first time. She was about Lee's height but very thin and her face was extremely pale with large circles under her eyes. Actually, she looked ill. Or perhaps she was just cold. Ruby felt ashamed of pulling away and squeezed her hand. 'I guess we're going to be very hot soon. A good thing too.'

'Good.' Nadire smiled as she pronounced the English word and Ruby smiled too. But she did think her new friend an odd choice for such a testing adventure. If she wasn't sick, she was certainly frail. It struck Ruby that for once, she herself was not the weakest physical specimen around.

'Did *you* see a card with red, green and yellow colours?' Ruby spoke very slowly and Nadire seemed to understand. At least she nodded.

'Where were you?' Again, Ruby said the words extra clearly and again Nadire seemed to understand. She made a square shape with her hands and indicated swirling colours. All the same, thought Ruby, it was quite an effort talking to someone who couldn't speak English and, just as she was thinking that, she heard an echo from the headmaster's words: 'It won't be easy for them, learning a new language, finding new friends . . .' Maybe that was what Nadire was about, maybe she was a real live refugee.

'I'll bet it'll be hot when we stop,' said Ruby, giving Nadire her biggest smile.

They were obviously in some kind of tropical latitude. On the island ahead, they could see a palm grove behind a sandy beach and behind that the darker rise of a mountain. Between the two there seemed to be fields and a winding track on which they could see a few people descending towards them.

'I should say it's about three miles across,' said Slate. 'But of course there's no way of telling how deep it goes.'

The boat began to slow and Raymond made them go into the cabin as they prepared to land, so they saw nothing more until the boat had tied up.

'Everyone out!' yelled Raymond at last and they piled to the side. And it turned out they were not tied up at all, but had dropped anchor in the bay and what they were expected to do was jump into the water and wade or swim in to the beach. The sea was absolutely calm but even so it was quite a challenge after a long night of travelling and all of them fully dressed.

'Do we take off our shoes?' asked Ruby, although she was actually worried about the depth of the water.

'Il faut nager. J'adore the swimming! Papa teach me when I a baby.'

Ruby watched, amazed, as St Ives, that little waif and stray, gave a merry smile and leaped over the side. He dropped down into the transparent water, leaving a trail of bubbles, before bobbing up again and shouting. 'It's not deep. Pas du tout. I must swim but you can walk.' He trod water, smiling and waving happily.

'What about our clothes?' Lee, who was as tall as anyone and, as Ruby knew, was in the swimming team at school, stood on the side of the boat looking shocked. 'They'll be ruined.'

'Water never ruined anything.' Cherie had come up beside her. 'Just take off your jackets. Salt water cleanses all our impurities and the sun dries our good strong skins in a moment.'

Ruby watched as Lee followed Slate overboard. Gingerly they lowered themselves into the water, followed by the other children, except for Nadire, of course, who was staying close by her. St Ives swam round them like a fish. The trouble was they were all much taller than her and her swimming skills were almost nil and what if her glasses fell in the water and disappeared under the sand, and that left out what her mother would say if her clothes came back stiff with salt. She sat down on the deck dismally, feeling very unadventurous indeed. Nadire sat beside her.

'Darlings, you two come with me.' Ruby felt Cherie's hand, pulling her up. 'We'll float in with the baggage.' At the back of the boat an inflatable rubber raft had been blown up and was now being loaded by Raymond and his crew. 'Get in first,' commanded Cherie, 'and we'll put in the rest round you.'

So Ruby sailed to shore on the rubber raft and arrived just as the others came splashing in. Slate came running to her, sand flying up from his bare feet. 'Isn't this like far out, man, like, like . . .' words seemed to fail him before he had inspiration, 'like stepping into a TV commercial!'

'So where's the ice-cold drink then?' Lee joined them. They all stood round, their clothes dripping, shivering a little even though the sun was scorching hot, and wondering what happened next. Only St Ives seemed completely untroubled. He had taken all his clothes off, except his underpants, and was waving them around like flags.

'Hats on!' Cherie appeared. At least they guessed it was her by her voice since she had become invisible under a straw hat with wide brim in front and a flap decorated with ribbons behind. Once they had unpacked their hats and St Ives had at least partially re-dressed himself, they set off from the beach. Slate walked with Ruby, and Nadire dropped behind them, although Ruby could feel her eyes on her back.

'She never leaves me for a moment,' she whispered in case Nadire's English suddenly improved.

'Yeah,' Slate seemed uninterested. 'You're like her only friend, I guess.'

'Thanks for a hole in the wall,' moaned Ruby. 'She's just so depressing. Those big sad eyes. The trouble is I think she may be a refugee.'

'I'm worried about Cedric and Aurora,' said Slate, making no comment about whether Nadire was or wasn't a refugee.

'Where are they?' In all the excitement Ruby had quite forgotten about them.

'Didn't you see? Aurora flew straight inland from the boat and I haven't seen her since Cedric slithered off that raft you came in on, and now he's bunked off too.'

'I expect they're finding friends,' Ruby looked up. They were passing through the palm grove and above her head she could hear squawking and chattering and caught a flash of red and yellow.

'I don't know.' Slate peered up anxiously. 'A city-bred pigeon on a tropical island. Brent will kill me if anything happens to her. She's a brilliant racing pigeon.'

'I thought she was a dove,' said Ruby vaguely. She was interested that despite all his protestations about not caring if he never went back, he was worried about home too. 'I bet I'm more out of place than Cedric or Aurora.' Ruby suddenly felt filled with self-pity. 'Look, I'm sweating so much my glasses are sliding down my nose. Soon, they'll be completely misted over and I won't be able to see a thing.'

'I'm cool. You should have waded in. It was a good laugh.'

'My legs are too short.' Fearing she was about to cry, she turned away from him. 'And I'm such a bad swimmer, I'd certainly have drowned.'

'I'll tell you something if you don't make it public news.' Slate paused. 'I can't swim at all.'

Ruby was enjoying being consoled when a loud scream made them both swing round. It was Lee, screeching and flailing her arms about, but oddly not moving her feet at all. Nadire was already there, standing sympathetically, hunched and silent.

Ruby, St Ives and Slate rushed to her side. 'On my foot!' she yelled. 'I'm probably going to be stung to death! There're thousands of them! Hundred of thousands! Don't just stare! Do something!' They looked down and then jumped backwards as they saw a broad band of large black ants flowing over Lee's foot.

Raymond caught up with them and put down the bags which had festooned his arms, shoulders and back. 'You've terrified them,' he commented calmly. And since Lee merely stared with wide-open eyes, he continued, 'Look how fast they're crossing the path.'

'Over my foot,' quavered Lee. 'My *bare* foot.'

'As far as they're concerned, it's just a bit of the path. Cutter ants are very intelligent, but within limits. If they get too frightened, they'll sting.'

This thought completely silenced Lee. To be stung by hundreds and thousands of ants certainly did not appeal.

'Just keep still and let them pass,' continued Raymond. They all watched, and the flow of ants seemed to go on for hours. Nadire took Lee's hand which none of the rest of them would have done. 'There. Emergency over!' exclaimed Raymond as the last ant scurried away into the undergrowth. 'Now. Who's for breakfast?'

The thought of food made them all dash forward until they left the jungly darkness to cross an open expanse of ground, almost white under the dazzling brightness of the sun. Ahead of them they saw a large round structure, open-sided but roofed with palm-leaf matting. It was on a steepish rise and a cool breeze blew through it. Tables were laid out with pale-coloured drinks in glass jugs, strange fruits piled high on oval dishes and rice and cous-cous in earthenware bowls. Two or three long silver fish decorated with limes stared balefully with round eyes. On a separate table there were twenty or more coconuts with bamboo straws sticking out of them. Around the edge of the building there were benches, strung with bristly string which in design were halfway to being hammocks. In between all this, Cherie darted about encouraging and explaining. 'Coconut milk is as unlike ordinary milk as beer is to wine,' she explained to a bewildered Nadire who was sitting so close to Ruby that she could hardly eat – although Nadire herself was using her fingers to eat ferociously.

'She doesn't speak English,' Ruby told Cherie while Nadire licked her fingers and gave her a grateful smile.

'She will soon, darling,' cried Cherie. 'Anything and everything is possible on this island,' she added before darting off to stand on a podium in the middle of the hut. 'This is our dome,' she shouted above the excited chattering. 'This is where we meet, where we eat, where we talk, listen and learn. This is the centre of our life here.' By now, everybody had drawn closer and was listening carefully.

For the first time, everything was quiet and settled and the children could look round at each other, to see how many boys there were and how many girls and what sort of kids: friendly, stuck-up, fat, thin, tall, short, posh-looking or like anyone else. Ruby looked and counted the numbers as she had on the aeroplane. But the strange thing was that, although she thought she was staring very hard or anyway quite as hard as usual, she somehow couldn't get quite beyond herself, Slate, Lee, Nadire and St Ives. There were fifteen other kids there; she could count them. But whenever she tried to pin them down a bit more, check whether they had fair hair or long noses or something odder, they seemed to shift out of focus and go all blurry as if they weren't absolutely one hundred per cent sitting there.

'Can *you* see what the other kids are like?' she whispered to Slate.

'Normal to grey,' answered Slate in a 'what a stupid question' voice.

But that was exactly it, thought Ruby, they were not only out of focus but grey or greyish too, a bit like shadows. She was leaning over to whisper to Lee when Cherie frowned in her direction and began to speak.

'You will see other smaller domes dotted about. When you have finished eating, separate yourselves into fives and choose a dome. Your packs are here. It'll be midday soon – no time to be outside. You'll know midday, incidentally, by the sun being directly overhead.'

Ruby looked at Slate who was sitting on her other side from Nadire and knew they were both thinking the same thing: Cherie needed to tell them how to tell the time by the sun because their watches had stopped. They had entered a whole other world, completely remote from the way they'd lived before. This made her think of something else, but before she dared speak, St Ives had shot up his hand.

'Please, mademoiselle, where are the toilettes?' Ever since swimming he had been so happy as to be irrepressible.

'A hundred yards north-east of the domes,' answered Cherie, to an audible sigh of relief from just about everyone.

'But mind you shut the door or the monkeys will come in with you. And while I'm on the subject of monkeys, never leave anything out of your pack or it'll be whipped up to the top of the tallest tree.'

It was easy enough for Ruby and Slate to group into five: Slate, Ruby plus the inevitable Nadire, Lee and St Ives. The greyishness of the other children didn't seem to matter. They were both there and not there and their real busy life was with each other. They went off together and with only a little arguing. (Lee was worried about the monkeys.) They settled on a dome on the edge of the jungle. 'It will be cooler,' said Ruby who was still suffering from heat. She'd finally had to tape her glasses to her head to stop them sliding down her nose.

Their beds, it turned out, were just like the string benches in the Central Dome. 'Very airy,' said Ruby, testing one.

'Good,' said a voice at her side.

Ruby looked at Nadire. She had stayed close to her all day but of course they hadn't been able to speak, so apart from this feeling that she must be a refugee she hadn't a clue about her background. She knew absolutely nothing about her. The others treated her as if she didn't exist at all which was certainly typical of the selfishness of Slate and Lee. So Ruby had to be the one to look after her.

'Will your parents be worried about you?' She spoke slowly, saying the first thing she thought of.

As usual Nadire seemed to understand more than she could speak. Perhaps Cherie was right and she'd soon be rattling away in English. Nadire shook her head. 'No parents. Only aunt. We refugees.'

'I guessed that!' exclaimed Ruby. 'But you've got parents? Back home, I mean.'

Nadire shook her head again but more energetically so that her pale straight hair whisked across her face. 'No home. Mother sick. In my country. No father. All gone.'

Ruby could think of nothing else to ask and was glad to be interrupted by Lee who thought she had seen a monkey trying to steal her tooth brush.

'Nadire's a refugee,' Ruby told her reprovingly. After all, even she must see that losing your home must be a lot worse than losing your tooth brush.

But the truth is they were all too sleepy to think properly about anything. Slate was already flat out on his bed, eyes shut, even snoring a little.

'It is hot,' Ruby yawned.

'Very hot,' agreed Nadire and they both lay down thankfully.

When they awoke, a golden light was filtering under the palm thatch roof and from somewhere not too far away, they could hear a booming noise like a gong.

Ruby looked round and saw that everyone was rising

sleepily, having realised that must be a call to a meeting. As if in a dream, she staggered across to the Central Dome. The air was cooler, if not fresher, and she opened her eyes enough to see other figures coming from various directions. They sat either on the string benches or on the rather sandy floor. Suddenly, it was as if a brightness filled the middle of the circle they had made and Frederick and April Whipple stood in front of them.

'Are they real?' exclaimed Lee who, of course, had never seen them before.

'As real as you and me,' whispered Ruby, defensively, although she had to admit to herself that 'real' was hardly the word. Frederick was wearing a multi-coloured striped robe with a gold band round his black hair while April was wrapped in layers of silvery gauze clipped together with twinkling turquoise and pink brooches. Really, it was quite dazzling and, frankly, not in very good taste. You might call it vulgar or even laughable. She was sure Lee's mother would have called it that.

The gong stopped booming and Frederick and April began to speak, one after the other, taking turns.

'Welcome to the Island. Today we rest, tomorrow your new life begins.'

'This island is ours. It is yours. But it is also others'. We have the front of the island. The Others have the back.'

'Our island has wild blue sea, sandy beaches, a jungle filled with butterflies and monkeys, palm tree groves and clear freshwater springs.'

'The part of the island belonging to the Others has a stark, rocky coastline with sudden drops and dangerous gorges. It is a barren place with little shade except in dark caves dug into the hillside.'

'If you get to the Others' side, you will find it hard to return.'

There was a pause. Ruby and Slate looked at each other. 'Who are "the Others"?' moutherd Ruby.

'How do we know when we reach the Others' part of the island?' whispered Slate.

But neither question was answered because Frederick and April had gone and the word spread about that this was swimming time and then afterwards they would be shown a waterfall which was like the most glorious shower in the world.

Chapter Ten

Hearing and Seeing

Ruby would never forget the first night on the Island. The waterfall had been quite a long walk into the interior of the Island, so that when they came back the only light to show them the path, which wound through tall ferns and fan-like palms, was the brilliant moon. The air was very soft and filled with gentle flutterings and twitterings. Back at their dome, they lay in the darkness, talking quietly about what they had seen and what they might expect to see the next day. None of them talked or even thought of the world they had left behind. Home, if not exactly forgotten, seemed totally unimportant. It was as if they had been removed to a different time zone where they had a chance to be something new too.

In the morning, not long after dawn, they set off once more for the sea. The sun was still pale, the sea the colour of the turquoise brooches on April's dress. The evening before, Ruby had not gone further than her ankles, but now she found herself up to her waist in the clear water and from there it seemed the easiest thing in the world to lie backwards and find she was floating, hair spread about her like seaweed, arms wide, eyes fixed on the blue immensity above her.

'You swim!' cried a high-pitched voice beside her, accompanied by so much splashing that, for fear of being submerged, she stood abruptly.

'I was floating,' she told St Ives.

'You swim on your back. And Slate also. And now Nadire.'

Ruby stood up and looked about her. She had carefully tucked her glasses inside her shoes on the edge of the sea. But the extraordinary thing was that as she gazed at the sparkling waves where her friends swam and jumped and floated (there was Slate on his back, eyes closed and Nadire looking remarkably relaxed), as she turned to face the pale haze where the sea met the sky, she seemed to be seeing as sharply as if she *were* wearing her glasses. She remembered how the same thing had happened at the Salvation Army hall when Cherie had removed her glasses.

She turned round to look at the Island. There was the sandy beach, the thick trees, the large dome and some of the smaller ones. Behind were all the irregularities of the lower slopes of the Island. She thought she could pick out the ferny glen and the waterfall they had visited the night before. Further away, the land rose sharply to the rocky crags which separated the front of the island from the back. A small dark cloud appeared suddenly from behind the highest crag. Ruby shivered violently and turned back quickly to the cheerful beach scene.

'I can see perfectly,' she said almost to herself. But Lee bobbed up beside her just then.

'Don't be silly,' she said scornfully, 'you're blind as a bat.'

'I can swim too,' said Ruby, obstinately.

'You're just so *stupid*. If you can see better, it's because the light's bright and, if you can float, it's because the sea's so salty. Don't you know *anything*?'

Ruby stared at her with new clear eyesight and saw that Lee should never have been allowed on this trip. She had not changed at all from the old supercilious, cutting Lee. The words came into Ruby's head, 'She does not believe.'

'Why are you staring at me like that?' Lee looked even more irritable as Ruby made no attempt to answer, but flopped back again into the water. This time she let her face go right under. Eyes open, she watched glistening bubbles race past. It seemed she had lost all fear of the water. When she surfaced again, everybody was heading back to land, wading, splashing, jumping. She joined Nadire.

'How are you?' she asked slowly.

Nadire looked at her sideways. She had high cheekbones, widely spaced grey eyes and fine straight hair. Ruby suddenly realised that despite her extreme thinness, she was rather beautiful. 'I am like good,' she answered seriously.

Ruby laughed. Nadire was obviously learning her English from Slate. 'I am so glad you're here,' she said.

'Yes. I am too. It is like a dream.' Nadire stopped and looked down at the little waves flurrying at her feet. 'Here with you I do not feel alone. In England I feel alone. I am with my aunt. Not real aunt. She not want me. She goes. I have no one.'

'You speak wicked English!' exclaimed Ruby because Nadire's story was so sad and she didn't know what to say. She thought how odd it was that they all had parent problems. Nadire and St Ives were orphans, Slate had no mother and his brother seemed to take the place of his father while she had a mother all right and, on the whole, a great deal too much of her!

'How did you get here? I mean, did you see a strange card?'

'In room with many beds I see card. Just me sees. For me. Then a taxi come to bring doctor but no doctor. Just Cherie.'

'So there was no audition for you. Or perhaps you passed it even before you came to England.' Ruby looked at Nadire thoughtfully, but she was interrupted by Slate prodding her in the back and shouting.

'Come on, you two! Hurry. Hurry.' He was right to be urging them on. They were going to their first class in the Audition for Life programme. As they walked up, Ruby noticed that Nadire was no longer hugging so close to her, as if the swim and their conversation had given her new confidence. There was even some colour in her cheeks.

The big dome felt cool after the hot sun outside. A cold breeze made some palm fronds, turned upside down and dangling from the ceiling, wave to and fro like fans. Frederick and April were almost in darkness, issuing commands to Cherie who passed them on to the children.

First they were told to sit cross-legged on the floor. Then they were told to keep completely silent and listen. At first Ruby thought there was nothing to hear, but as the silence went on, her ears began to be crowded with noise; the wind came first, then the sea, a distant undertone, then the birds, although she couldn't tell one from the other, some making raucous noises, perhaps parrots or cockatoos, others making softer, sweeter sounds. She was sure that among them, she could hear Aurora's soft trilling. So the bird was safe then.

'How long does this go on?' whispered Slate beside her.

'Sssh!' Ruby was severe. She had just heard another layer of sound, the insects, some shrill, others only vibrating in the air.

'I can hear the monkeys,' whispered Lee, shivering nervously.

'Sssh,' said Ruby again. And this time she shut her eyes. It seemed to make her ears even sharper so that she felt as if she could hear sounds from all over the Island, even to the very back of it. Strange low grunts and hard, sharp barks came from far away, a threatening, ugly background to the other gentler sounds. She opened her eyes quickly to make them go away.

All around her, the other children were sitting with closed eyes. Slate's mouth was open with concentration, Nadire held her head in her hands, St Ives had a slight smile, Lee's head was tipped backwards. How strange they all looked! And, even stranger, as Cherie beat the gong, and all their eyes flashed open in surprise.

Ruby saw April and Fredrick smile at the sight and then whisper to Cherie.

'That is the end of your first lesson, my darlings,' pronounced Cherie before April raised her elegant hand.

'You have all listened. You have heard more than you have ever heard before. Do not lose those sounds.'

Frederick took over, 'Now you may play. But this afternoon when the gong sounds, you will return here and learn to see.' Then they were both gone, merged into the brightness of the tent.

'Like this is a good laugh,' said Slate to Lee in a loud mocking voice. And Lee laughed back as if she couldn't care less. But Ruby had seen them with their eyes shut and knew they were taking it all as seriously as her.

After another delicious lunch, they were allowed to

go for a swim. Strangely, since the morning's listening exercise, they all seemed to be hearing things they'd never heard before. While they were swimming, St Ives insisted he could hear fish talking. 'Like une souris, a little mouse,' was the way he described it. 'They were speaking in French,' he added. 'so you wouldn't understand.' Then his face became very still, his blue eyes half closed as if he were listening even more intently than before. 'Ah, the great fish!' he exclaimed, as if to himself.

Treading water, he turned to the horizon. 'Regardez. Look now!'

They all looked where he was pointing and saw shapes silhouetted on the horizon, rising from the water one after the other, leaping and diving in graceful arcs.

'Dolphins!' Ruby was impressed. Lee and Slate and Nadire watched, open-mouthed.

'Like, man, they're coming closer.' Slate was right. The leaping arcs were certainly bigger than before. Now they could see glittering water spraying off their shiny backs.

'They come to play.' St Ives spoke dreamily, not at all like his usual lively self. 'Once, not long before they die, Poppy and Hubert, Maman et Papa, take me to America. There is a big water there and dolphins. I go in and swim with a dolphin. I love my dolphin. I think this is my friend come to find me. Perhaps he takes me to mes parents.'

Lee and Ruby exchanged a look of anxiety, expressed in words whispered by Slate, 'I guess he's losing it.'

They waded towards St Ives, prepared to take him to the shore and comfort him. But he was already swimming away from them, too rapidly for any of them, even Lee who tried hardest, to catch him up.

'He's heading for the dolphins!' she cried.

'And they're heading for him,' added Ruby under her breath. But there was nothing any of them could do but stand in the clear water with their toes wriggling in the sand, and watch.

Soon it became obvious that one of the dolphins had separated itself from the rest and was coming directly for St Ives. They could see his face with its wet curls, bobbing along.

'He swims like a pro,' said Slate, sounding rather jealous.

'They lived in a caravan by the sea. He told us.'

'Look! Look!'

In the few seconds they had looked away, the dolphin and St Ives had met, two faces bobbing together as in a kiss, and then they were speeding round together, the little boy so close to the fish that they seemed one moving streak. Under the hot blue sky, they described a wide circle, a long white wake stretching behind them. Round they went a second time and then a third.

'Like a water rocket,' breathed Ruby.

'Speed boat, stupid,' argued Lee.

'He's dropped off!' shouted Slate, while Nadire just watched, hands together as if she were praying.

Now the dolphin was moving away from them, back

to join the others, who were still bounding and leaping near the horizon. The whole extraordinary episode had taken no longer than a few minutes.

St Ives swam slowly towards them. He was panting rather and as he got nearer, they could see the serious expression on his face.

'Are you OK?' asked Lee.

'Wow, man, cool!' exclaimed Slate, 'like the original boy with a dolphin.'

'He talked to me,' said St Ives and then swam directly to shore where he flopped on to the sand.

They all followed, running through the water so that spray spumed around their legs, and they knelt round the little figure.

'He talked to you . . .' prompted Lee.

St Ives put his hands behind his head and addressed the high blue sky. 'He told me he couldn't take me to Poppy and Hubert because the car crash killed them. But he said, they are happy now and they want me to be happy aussi so I must not go back to that school or to Grand-mère. This a début.' He paused for a moment, before sitting up and staring at them intently, as if it was important they understood. 'I listened to my friend, the dolphin so carefully. He spoke French. Début is beginning. I was happy with Maman and Papa. Now I shall be happy without them.'

'And never go back to that nasty school on the cliff!'

'Jamais!' shouted St Ives and, suddenly turning back

into the cheerful little boy they'd thought him before, he jumped to his feet. At which point, almost as if arranged, the gong began to sound from the Central Dome.

'Lesson number two,' grumbled Slate who was never very keen on learning and, certainly, they all felt reluctant to leave the sea. In the end it was St Ives who led them.

'J'écoute. I listen but I believe I not hear another dolphin.'

It was warm in the dome with very little breeze coming under the palm thatching. Their skin and eyes felt prickly from the salt water and they all felt in danger of going to sleep.

'Like where's the siesta?' asked Lee in her poshest voice. 'When we went on holiday to Italy – and it was nothing like as hot as this – we had a siesta every afternoon.'

'Well, I'm interested in seeing,' objected Ruby. 'With eyes like mine I need all the help I can get.'

Before anyone could comment, perhaps luckily, Cherie was bustling them to attention. 'Eyes open for this,' she cried, laughing at the joke of it.

And there, standing in front of them, yet not quite real, were Frederick and April.

'Do you see us?' they asked in unison, their voices vibrating in the hot air. 'Tell us what you see!'

'We see you!' chorused the children.

And, of course, they saw them. Considering April was dressed in gold lace over a red satin undergarment and Frederick wore mostly gold too but with some black here

92

and there it would have been hard not to see them – so Ruby thought.

'Do you see us?' repeated Frederick and April in their thrilling voices and all the children began to answer.

'We see . . .' But first one and then another broke off. They could see gold all right, but was it April's gold lace or was it the afternoon sunshine piercing through the palm roof and making lacy patterns on the floor? And things were no easier with Frederick. Again, there was plenty of gold, but the black looked more like dark shadows than trousers. Or had his trousers been gold?

'Can you see them?' whispered Ruby to Slate, thinking perhaps it was her bad eyes that made everything seem so vague.

'Like . . .' Slate paused, 'Like wavery. Like, I don't know. Like I can't see clearly at all.'

'It's the heat,' muttered Lee.

'Where are the faces?' asked Nadire and they all thought she was quite right. Where were the faces?

'Can you see us?' repeated Frederick and April.

'We can hear you!' chorused the children.

Once more Frederick and April spoke together. 'But you can't tell us apart from the hot sunlight and the palm leaf shadows . . .' Their voices crooned and slid over the air. 'It is beginning to feel as if you're asleep and in a dream. Dreaming . . .'

Ruby, eyes half-closing, thought that was exactly how it felt, and she felt, more than she saw, that everybody was feeling peculiar too, nodding, dozing, eyes only partly open. There was no way of knowing how long this strange state lasted, whether it was just minutes or whether it was hours and they really had fallen asleep.

The next thing they knew was the gong beaten urgently, bringing them to full attention. Frederick and April now stood clearly in front of them.

'You *see*,' said April, emphasising the word and smiling gently, as if she sympathised with their problem of seeing and not seeing. 'We wanted you to understand that you cannot always believe the evidence of your own eyes.'

'What *seems* to be there,' continued Frederick, also kindly, 'may not be what it seems or may not be there 'at all.'

'The eye,' continued April, smiling, 'is not to be trusted.'

'And that is the end of the lesson.' Frederick had become stately so that Ruby was reminded of her headmaster – although the idea of Mr Harpsden in gold lace and black satin made her giggle to herself. By the time she had got over that image, Frederick and April had vanished in a final sort of way and Cherie was back, advising them that it was time to revisit the waterfall.

'Let's hope the waterfall's still there,' commented Lee in her mocking voice. Ruby refused to laugh. What this afternoon's lesson had made her realise was that wearing glasses was not the most important part about the way you saw things. This made her feel very happy.

Chapter Eleven

Kidnapped

Ruby had no idea what woke her. The darkness was so intense she felt she could put out her hand and touch it. In fact she did put out her hand, but what she touched was Aurora, sleeping by her side, her feathers soft as silk. It was then she heard a high-pitched yelp, an animal, she assumed – and then was not so sure. And then when it came again, she was quite certain it wasn't.

'Lee,' she whispered. 'Lee!' No answer. Before she got out of her bed and over to Lee's, she knew the answer. It was Lee who had cried out. She had disappeared into the blackness. 'Slate!' Now Ruby's voice was loud enough to wake everybody. 'Slate, Lee's gone! She's really gone. I heard a scream.'

In a moment, they were all out of bed, gathered anxiously in the darkness. There was, of course, no electric light and in their anxiety, they couldn't find matches for the candles. Even so, there was just enough light from the moon to make out that Cedric was slung about Slate's neck like a long scarf.

'Do you think she's really gone?' worried Ruby, repeating her own words. After yesterday's lesson in seeing and believing, anything seemed possible.

'Mais le cri!' St Ives seemed more excited than anxious.

'Yeah. Like, you heard a scream,' Slate stroked Cedric's neck thoughtfully.

'Kidnapped.' Nadire's eyes were big and dark in the moonlight. 'She is kidnapped. This is not monkey play. This is danger.'

They all looked at each other. Nadire seemed to have a way of pin-pointing the truth. Then Aurora who hadn't cooed once, as if impressed by the seriousness of the occasion, began to flutter her wings. The noise seemed loud in the silence. Yes, thought Ruby, they must take action.

'We must go and get help from the Central Dome,' Slate said. Again his voice seemed unnaturally loud. 'From April and Frederick. They will know what to do.'

Secretly relieved that he didn't suggest dashing into the night after Lee, Ruby agreed at once, although St Ives, who was definitely the bravest, had to be restrained from making himself a one-man rescue party.

Staying very close together, they set off across the flat, rather sandy ground that lay between their own dome and the Central Dome. They knew they were going the right way because they could hear the noise of the sea through the trees on their right.

It was Nadire who, with her ever-improving English, once again said what was in all their minds, 'We are too far. The dome was there, behind. It has gone.'

'Don't be silly,' explained Ruby, firmly, although actually she felt near tears. 'We've just gone in the wrong direction.'

'Like going in circles, man,' contributed Slate. 'Cool it, Nadire.'

Ruby and St Ives looked at him reproachfully.

'I am not cool,' said Nadire, 'when Lee is kidnapped.'

'Gone,' said Slate, 'that's all we know.'

They walked more. At least St Ives, who seemed able to see in the dark, ran, returning from wider and wider forays to report that there was nothing out there, no Central Dome at all and, even odder, he couldn't find either of the three other smaller domes which, like theirs, had been positioned only a few hundred yards from the main dome.

'Don't be silly,' said Ruby again but her voice sounded weak. By now a faint light was rising to the right of the mountain at the back of the island. It became stronger and they could see each other's strained, pale faces. There was no sign of the dome. Nobody said anything.

Ruby remembered the strange way this whole adventure had started. Why should they be so surprised – and yet it had all seemed so real. She blinked. Not *seemed* real, it had *been* real. Again, she remembered yesterday's lesson in seeing and not seeing.

'So where's everybody else?' asked Slate.

They looked at each other even more blankly. It was a fair question. There was absolutely no sign of the other winners in the Audition for Life. No domes, no people. No children, no Cherie, no Raymond, no boat crew, no Frederick or April.

'I wonder. Do we have a boat?' murmured Nadire.

They ran, at once – for the moment, quite forgetting Lee – through the trees and out on to the beach. There was not one boat but two. A small one pulled up on the sand, a boat with two paddles, wooden and painted a cheerful turquoise. They were sure they had not seen that before. Further out, in the deeper, bluer water, a white motor boat bobbed up and down, anchored somewhere in the ocean.

'Wicked!' exclaimed Slate with relief.

Wicked was the word for it. They could leave the island any time they wanted. There remained one problem. 'What about Lee?' said Ruby, gloomily.

They all flopped on the sand, too disheartened even to notice how inviting the little waves were, rippling across the sand. Without Lee, of course they could not leave the island.

A good five or even ten minutes passed before anyone

said another word. Eventually, Ruby managed to put into words something which had been hovering in her mind. 'I think it may be a sort of test,' she said.

'Like heavy, man.' This appeared to be Slate's way of agreeing.

'I'm not saying I understand . . .' Ruby rolled over on to her stomach.

'It's to help us with our lives, I think, and there are tests and learning for all of us.' Nadire stood up. 'I think that's what this funny Audition for Life means.' She looked towards the mountain made darker by the sun which was rising behind it and, all the time, growing in brightness and warmth.

'We must set off straight away.' St Ives bounced to his feet.

'Before it gets too hot,' said Ruby. She stared at the sand, despite her sensible advice, quite prepared to count every grain before setting off on what would certainly be a terrifying expedition. 'Why did Lee have to come?' she mumbled. 'She didn't even pass the audition.' But everybody else seemed filled with energy, although Slate looked distinctly less enthusiastic when he realised there was no prospect of breakfast.

'I suppose no food is like another kind of test,' he said, gloomily. 'At least I get chips at home, or rather in the chip shop.'

'We eat wild fruits.' Nadire sounded remarkably unfazed at the prospect. 'When we live in the forest, after we leave home, we eat all sorts of wildness.'

Ruby thought everything was more fantastic than ever. No wonder Nadire was so thin if she had lived off wild fruits. Very slowly she got to her feet. She must show a bit of mettle too.

'We must go to the waterfall first,' she said. 'You can survive for ages without food so long as you have water.'

The waterfall seemed different from the day before, the shady bushes darker, the water colder, the drop fiercer. They drank from their cupped hands which was not satisfactory, the liquid sliding through their fingers.

'I am sure, like there were coconuts on those palm trees,' said Slate. 'They have milk in them, don't they?' But it was too late to go back.

'We'll have them for supper,' suggested Ruby. And she thought to herself, If we ever get back.

They emerged into the sunlight again, now very hot and strong, and started across the plain of scrubby grasses which led to the steep rocky incline and the back of the island. The grasses were sharp-edged and soon Nadire, who was wearing a skirt, had red stripes criss-crossing her legs.

'Don't they hurt?' asked Ruby.

'Just a little.' They all stopped as Slate, looking embarrassed, took off his T-shirt and tore it open so that Nadire could wrap it around her legs. Ruby looked at Slate's torso and hoped his darker skin would not burn as easily as hers. Even though every part of her body was covered and she was wearing a hat, she still felt as if her skin was on fire. Not for the first time, she wondered why she'd had the bad luck to be born a redhead.

It took several hours to cross the unshaded plain, although, since all their watches had stopped, they could only tell the time by the sun which soon was directly above their heads. In all that time they saw no animals, but several times the dry grasses rustled only a few yards from where they were as if something was moving nearby, perhaps watching them.

Once, St Ives dashed over very quickly and, with a lot of hand waving, described seeing the tail of a long golden snake as it slithered away. But nobody quite believed him. 'Cedric would come and join us and not act like a spying stranger,' objected Slate who had not seen the snake for some time and was trying to hide his concern.

'A very very big snake would make un bruit comme that.' St Ives, smaller than the rest, found the going hard and was bright red in the face, his yellow curls dark with sweat. 'A serpent gigantesque!'

'Or a lion or a tiger,' added Slate, out of the corner of his mouth.

'Or a boar or a buffalo,' began Ruby, but at just that moment she had the most horrible sensation inside the legs of her jeans. For a moment she couldn't even scream.

'Aaeegh!' Ruby's screams brought everyone to a complete stop. 'Ah! Ah! Ah!' she began to beat at her jeans with her hands. Nadire was there first. She remained calm.

'Spiders,' she said. 'Please. Quiet. Perhaps they not bite.'

But Ruby was dancing around, almost breathless in her panic. 'They're inside my jeans . . .' Her voice was hardly more than a gasp.

'Take off,' Nadire took Ruby's arm to hold her still. Slate and St Ives watched open-mouthed as Nadire carefully rolled off the jeans. The spiders were about an inch across, black and furry with far too many legs to count. Ruby now stood completely still with her eyes squeezed tight shut. She thought that if she looked down and actually saw the spiders on her skin she would probably die of terror. I will simply pretend they're not there, she told herself, and now yesterday's lesson turned out to have a practical application. I'll pretend that this terrible tickling as nasty furry legs crawl up my skin is just not happening.

'They look like, like ink splodges,' whispered Slate in an awed voice, as Nadire carefully picked off the first one. 'Ruby's skin is so white it could be paper.'

'They're not there,' said Ruby between clenched teeth. 'And if they are there – which they're not – they aren't biting.'

'Comme elle est courageuse!' exclaimed St Ives.

Guessing 'courageuse' meant 'brave', Ruby felt cheered. Perhaps she was not a puny, blind, red-haired shrimp. Perhaps she was brave and even 'courageuse'.

'Merci,' she thanked him, although still keeping her eyes tight shut.

'Two more,' said Nadire, picking away. Meanwhile, Slate, with rather less enthusiasm than Nadire, was picking the spiders off the jeans. As each one was dropped to the ground, it scuttled away into some unseen hole. 'I think like they're scared too,' commented Slate. At last they were all gone and Ruby dared open her eyes and look down at her legs which were as usual, apart from a tracery of thin red claw marks.

'Oh, Nadire!' Ruby hugged her gratefully. 'Without you I would have died.'

'No. No. You are good strong girl.'

So Ruby, feeling very brave and strong, put her jeans back on and forwards they went, Ruby and Nadire arm in arm.

The sun was higher than ever and therefore hotter. Ahead of them the far edge of the grassland they were crossing seemed like a mirage, never getting closer. But at last the tall grasses became sparser and they felt cooler air reaching out towards them.

Thankfully, they hurried over the last few yards and at last were under the shadow of a belt of tall trees.

'Like groovy!' rejoiced Slate and they were all about to collapse on the ground when the peaceful shade turned into a wild scene of noise and movement.

CHAPTER TWELVE

The Others

Hundreds of monkeys, screeching and chattering, were streaming down the tree trunks, before bounding down and running towards them. Some had their teeth bared in a ferocious snarl, others had baby monkeys clinging to their stomachs. Nevertheless, they were just as aggressive as the males.

Ruby remembered Cherie warning them against the monkeys, but she had never suggested they would attack. The little ones round the domes had been more like playthings, not frightening at all. But these ones were bigger than she was! Somehow it made it worse that they looked more than halfway human, like bandy-legged jockeys, she thought.

'Don't run!' shouted Slate. He was quite right, of course, because where could they run to? Certainly not back across the boiling plain with the cutting grass. 'I'm going to, like eyeball him,' said Slate. The 'him' he referred to was a monkey, bigger than the rest, presumably a male, now no more than a metre from Slate. Ruby watched as Slate took a long stride towards him – they were about the same height – folded his arms and stared. The monkey stopped, black beady eyes fixed on Slate.

'He really is eyeballing him,' whispered Nadire. All the other monkeys had stopped behind their leader, although some still shouted and chattered excitedly.

'I'm going to clap my hands,' Slate said quietly, 'and I want you all to chant "Go home, go home, go home . . ."' Ruby and Nadire exchanged a glance. 'Go home', sounded a bit weak, to say the least. Slate slowly brought his hands together and suddenly there was a loud crack and then another and another.

'Coups de fusil!' cried St Ives as Slate looked utterly bewildered at his hands as if they could have produced such a sound.

'Gun shots,' murmured Nadire. The monkeys were not at all bewildered. Starting with their leader, they ran like crazy, now gibbering with fear and terror. In a few seconds, they had completely disappeared, cowering perhaps on the topmost branches of the trees.

'Good news, man,' said Slate, which was true in one

way; none of them fancied being torn apart by a herd of vengeful monkeys. On the other hand, where and who was the man – or men – with guns? Were they the Others who had kidnapped Lee and now were going to attack them? They waited uncertainly for a few moments until something crashed down from above their heads, and then more and more. Nadire and Ruby picked one up. Then another. Coconuts. The monkeys, not cowed for long, were using them as missiles.

'Forward. Like quickly,' said Slate. 'Or they'll be on us again.' Each taking a coconut, which seemed like an excellent menu for a late lunch, they ran through the coppice of trees until they came out the other side where the rocky mountain started almost immediately. Their exhilaration at escaping the monkeys made them start up a winding path until one by one, they collapsed, utterly exhausted.

It was quite cool where they lay, the mountain shaded the sun and, although the rock was warm, there was still enough grass growing for comfort. St Ives, after telling them about picnics with his parents when they'd dug for crabs in the sand, began to crash his coconut against a stone. The moment it broke, he drank any milk which hadn't drained away with a look of ecstasy. Then he dug out the white flesh with a pointed stone. Soon they were all doing the same.

'And to think I always told my mum I hated coconuts!' exclaimed Ruby.

Only Slate continued to look anxious. He was thinking

of the gunshots. Slate knew something about guns. Dogs and other animals weren't the only things collected in his house. Looked away in the cellar was a whole battery of guns. His brother kept them clean, but Slate was pretty certain he didn't use them. On the other hand, he knew his father had once. That's why he was away up north. That's why he was in prison. And that's why Slate took the sound of gunfire very seriously. He wanted to talk about it to Ruby, but when he had finished with his coconut, he saw that everybody else had settled down for a sleep, eyes shut, limbs sprawled and relaxed. He felt tensely awake.

Slate stood. He shivered a little which reminded him that while they were running, Nadire had taken off his shirt and then dropped it somewhere, near the edge of the trees. He could easily collect it. Torn or not, it would be better than nothing. Quietly, Slate set off down the path.

Ruby stirred and then woke abruptly. She saw the others had done the same, their faces were pale under the sunburn, their eyes not quite focused.

'Another gunshot!'

'Where's Slate?'

They spoke together, looked around wildly, jumped up and started to run down the path. That's where the shot had come from. Ruby was ahead and it was she who half saw, half heard, something being dragged away into the darkness of the trees.

'Slate!' she screamed.

'Slate! Slate! Slate!' screamed St Ives and Nadire behind her. But there was no answer and no Slate.

'Of course he's not dead,' said Nadire after a moment's silence because they each knew what the other was thinking. There was another moment's silence.

'It was a gun to make fear not to kill,' suggested St Ives with a very funny accent, except no one was laughing. 'They sound like real gun.' There was a third pause as Ruby and Nadire wondered how St Ives could possibly know what a gun that wasn't a real gun would sound like.

'It was a real gun,' said Nadire heavily. 'I know real guns. When they take my father, they shoot guns. My brother run. They shoot. So my father go and hide.'

Ruby put out her hand and took Nadire's. Nadire smiled at her. 'I sorry to make you sad.'

'Please. We're very very sorry for you and your family.' Ruby thought that normally she'd have hardly been able to take in Nadire's story about the death of her brother. It would seem too shocking, too remote. But the way things were at the moment, it just made her feel very close to Nadire. But now they must think of Slate.

'They'll have taken Slate to the other side of the mountain.' Ruby tried to sound as positive as possible. 'There must be a second path. Perhaps we don't have to go over the mountain. Perhaps we can go round it.'

'Or through it,' said Nadire. They hesitated, undecided, trying not to show quite how frightened they were. 'I don't know,' Nadire looked up with more determination, 'but I feel there is a way through. I *feel* it. Whoever they are, the people, the Others, who have taken Lee and Slate, they don't go over the mountain. We'd see them. We'd see them now. But they have gone into thin air. People who fire guns do not go into the thin air.'

'The mountain is not so big, après tout,' St. Ives began to get excited, almost jumping up and down. 'Perhaps they make a tunnel with dynamite. Boom! Boom! We must find a way in. Voilà!' He gave a very French flourish with his hand.

Ruby thought, but didn't say, What a pathetic rescue party: one little boy, one refugee and one short-sighted redhead, stupid and almost stunted. Then she remembered that she was brave and 'courageuse' and decided to stop thinking like that. 'We should start searching straight away,' she said. 'Before it's too dark.'

'C'est ça!' cried St Ives, excitedly.

'We will look for a shadow on the bottom of the mountain,' suggested Nadire.

'Or a tree that looks as if it might be camouflage for an entrance,' added Ruby.

'Wicked, man! Like this is living!'

Ruby and Nadire exchanged a look which meant, now St Ives is going to talk like Slate. All the same, they were glad of his enthusiasm. With the intent expressions that befitted a serious search party, they set off in a northward direction.

Chapter Thirteen

Inside the mountain

They found the entrance to the mountain an hour or two later. They had almost given up and Ruby was admiring a large bush covered in huge creamy flowers which seemed to glow in the dusk. Suddenly, she realised there was nothing behind them or rather a hole, a space, total blackness. She pushed past the flowers which gave out a strong sweet smell that made her feel rather sick (particularly on an empty stomach) and found herself in a tunnel, neatly cut into the stone with a flat earth floor. They had been whispering since Slate's disappearance so, instead of shouting, she went out and led Nadire and St Ives to the entrance.

'Allo!' St Ives' voice echoed round the stone vaulting. He lowered it to a whisper, 'It's assez dark, n'est ce pas?'

'I have matches.' Ruby and St Ives looked at Nadire with astonishment as she produced a box of matches from her skirt pocket. 'Always I carry matches. We leave our home in the autumn, and autumn becomes winter and we live in the forest. The mushrooms and berries first. Later snow and ice. Without matches we have no fire, we die of cold.'

Ruby and St Ives were too impressed to comment. Ruby thought that Nadire had already been through so many frightening adventures that she must think their present situation quite tame. 'Well, there's no point waiting around,' Ruby said eventually.

The matches did make their progress easier but not easy. Soon they realised that they'd use up the whole box very quickly if they lit them one after another. They walked in darkness, holding hands so that they didn't lose each other. After the brilliance and heat of the day, it was most disconcerting to find themselves surrounded by darkness and dank stone walls which had probably never seen sunlight.

Ruby felt her hand, which was holding on to St Ives', become colder and colder. Then, suddenly, she felt him pulling away from her. 'Where are you going?' she hissed.

'Down the tunnel.'

'Not that way.' They stopped and lit a match. Clearly this was an emergency. The tunnel divided in front of them, both openings were equal in size, but going different ways.

'Ouch!' exclaimed Nadire, as the match burnt her fingers. They were back in darkness again. Ruby took off her glasses and put them in her jeans' pocket. There was no point in wearing them when she couldn't see anything anyway.

'Au moins, it's not hot,' commented St Ives.

'Cold,' said Nadire. 'I freeze.'

'What we need,' said Ruby, 'is a guide.'

'Yes, we do!' agreed Nadire. 'I pray.'

They stood dismally, unable to choose which direction to take.

The sound was very soft at first, a slight cooing, a delicate fluttering.

'Aurora!' shouted Ruby, the word echoing down both tunnels and coming back again. Aurora was here to be their guide, she realised at once. Nadire's prayer had been answered. Having fluttered around them for a moment, she set off down the right-hand tunnel.

They followed gratefully, catching glimpses of a feathered whiteness, listening for the cooing when they could see nothing. They were all filled with hope again and continued quite briskly for as long as an hour until, quite without warning, they found themselves in a round chamber lit by natural light from a hole in the top. With a final chirrup Aurora flew out of this hole and disappeared.

'We must be near the end of the mountain,' said St Ives, longingly.

'It's the moon shining in,' said Nadire, who had been staring at the hole. 'It's night-time.'

Ruby reached for her glasses. Just before she put them on, with no warning at all, she was blinded and knocked to the floor. It was such a shock that at first she hardly realised that a massive jet of water, as powerful as a water cannon, had come straight through the hole and bowled her over. The chamber filled with water in a matter of seconds and were it not for the outlet tunnel they would all have been drowned.

'My glasses have gone! I can't swim!' yelled Ruby above the surging noise.

'Flottez! Float!' shrieked St Ives in his high-pitched voice. In fact the current of water was far too strong for anyone to swim. They were carried by it along the tunnel at breakneck speed until they were flung into the open air and found themselves in a large pond surrounded by dark shrubs.

'Out!' screamed Nadire. 'The water goes. Quick! Quick!' She was absolutely right. At the centre of the pond, there was a whirlpool just as if the plug had been removed from a bath, but of course the pull was far far stronger and the hole big enough to suck down a child.

'I can't swim!' repeated Ruby, already feeling herself being drawn to the centre.

'Yes, you can! Turn on your back and kick your legs,' commanded St Ives. 'We help you.'

As they struggled towards the bank, Ruby thought that if she survived this experience she would never ever be frightened of anything ever again. At last they reached the edge of the pond and, with the help of the shrubs, hauled themselves out. Utterly exhausted, they collapsed on the soft earth, as soft as the softest bed in the world, even if rather damp. They listened as with explosions, pops and gurgles, the last of the water shot down its giant plug-hole.

'Do you think it was a flash flood?' asked Nadire.

'Or was it directed at us?'

'The Others, you mean?' whispered St Ives.

'Yes, I do.' Ruby shivered violently and then sneezed. The air was quite cold on this shadowy side of the mountain, even if they hadn't been soaking wet which they were. And hungry. Now they were resting and quiet, their stomachs were making very angry sounds indeed. This has to be the worst moment, thought Ruby, and at that moment, things got much worse. There was a rustling sound in one of the thickets nearby and out of it flew dozens of black-winged creatures, hard, bony bodies with wings like kites, sharply angled and threatening.

'Ce sont des chauves-souris!' screamed St Ives. 'Monster bats.'

'My hair.' Ruby froze, arms above her head. 'They'll go for my hair!' Her monstrous mass of orange, tangled frizz. Since she was a child, her mother had warned her, 'You've a bat-catcher growing on your head, not normal hair at all. Just mind dark places in the night.' Hysterically, Ruby struggled out of her wet T-shirt and wound it round her head. Then she crouched down, cowering, eyes shut.

After several cowering, terrified minutes, she felt Nadire touch her shoulder. 'They've gone.' Ruby opened her eyes. Even without her glasses, she could see Nadire's worried frown. 'I see you hate your hair,' she said.

'Yes,' agreed Ruby, simply.

'Shall I cut it?'

Despite everything, Ruby almost laughed. 'Just like that?'

'I always carry scissors.'

So, there, in that strange tropical night, Nadire cut Ruby's hair. Orange frizz descended to the ground or was carried away on unseen air streams. After a while Nadire stood back and Ruby put her hand to her head. 'It feels so light!' she exclaimed wonderingly. 'I feel as if I could fly up to the stars.'

'I like it,' Nadire looked pleased with herself. 'It's like a neat cap of curls.'

'I feel like a new person,' rejoiced Ruby. 'No glasses. No hair.'

'No food, en plus,' added St Ives, gloomily, who had little interest in solving Ruby's hair problems.

By now their eyes had got used to the dark, blacker than ever since the moon had sailed away to the east side of the mountain. It was St Ives who noticed a new source of light, not very far away, a steady golden gleaming. 'Voilà! That's where they are!' he cried, triumphantly.

'They?' questioned Nadire.

'The Others,' answered Ruby.

It was true that none of them had really thought through what they were doing, they had merely set out to find Lee and then Slate.

'They have guns,' said Nadire. 'Do we walk to them and say, "Please, give us Lee and Slate. Thank you very much."?'

Ruby realised that was exactly what she had been planning to do. Everything about the whole expedition had been so strange that that had seemed as reasonable an idea as any other.

'You mean they might want to shoot us?' St Ives seemed rather excited at the prospect.

'We know nothing,' said Nadire. 'Maybe they are not so bad.' There was a pause while they all thought how unlikely that was.

'We must approach cautiously.' Ruby listened as her stomach rumbled like a train. 'We'll certainly starve to death if we stay here.'

'D'accord,' St Ives nodded energetically.

So they set off again, single file towards the light. After five or ten minutes, they began to smell the most delicious aromas of food cooking. Nadire smelled lamb stew with onions and carrots and turnips. St Ives smelled frog-legs with garlic sauce (which was a very sophisticated French taste) and Ruby smelled fruit salad with strawberries and peaches and ice cream on the side. In fact each of them smelled what they most enjoyed.

Soon they were close enough to see dark figures silhouetted against the lights. They stopped and tried to see each other's expressions.

'One of us should go forward,' whispered Ruby, eventually. Since neither of the other two said anything, she added, 'I will.' What was she doing, Ruby, the feeble, shy, girl, who usually (but not just now) wore glasses as thick as bottle bottoms, crawling along in the undergrowth, spying on potential murderers? It was yet another mystery. But there she was, on an unknown tropical island and close enough now to hear men and women's voices and, if she eeled forward another few yards, she'd be able to hear what they were saying.

CHAPTER FOURTEEN

The Pit

Like even the best plans there was a flaw in Ruby's bold thinking, and the flaw was that the group by the fire were speaking in a very very foreign language, all gutturals and '*ughs*' and '*humphs*'. There was no hope of understanding a word. Ruby was about to report back to Nadire and St Ives in despair when she realised she had just understood several words coming, however, from a different direction.

'Over here. Like to the left.' The voice came from outside the light cast by the fire. Slowly, Ruby crawled towards it.

'That's it,' whispered the voice, which quite obviously was Slate's, 'Like don't fall in.'

His warning came just in time. One of Ruby's feet was just sliding down a steep-sided hole when she flung herself backwards. She crouched on the edge, staring down, but only seeing blackness. 'Slate, is that you?'

'Sssh. Yeah. 'Course it's me. Lee's here too but she's asleep. I think they've put something funny into her drink. She's sleepy all the time.'

'Are you all right?'

'If you call being at the bottom of a massive great pit being all right. You've got to get a rope.'

'A rope?'

'To haul us out with.'

'Do they feed you?'

'Bread, fruit, chucked down. Coconuts. Not exactly burgers and chips.'

It struck Ruby that she and Nadire and St Ives would enjoy the bread and fruit but on the other hand they weren't stuck down a hole, being drugged. 'Why have they captured you? And who are they?'

'Negative. I've never even seen their faces. I don't know anything. I just think of them as the Others like Frederick and April said.' Slate suddenly sounded very tired. His voice seemed further away as if he'd laid down. 'Just hurry up and get us out of here before we find out what they want.'

'Cool,' said Ruby, to cheer him up, and went off to find the others. At first they were so excited they were ready to dash straight back to the pit until they remembered the need for a rope.

'You could hold mes pieds. Ruby and Nadire could hold yours and . . .'

'Feet,' corrected Ruby irritably. 'That's a terrible idea. We'd all end up in the pit.'

'So much gourmet food,' murmured St Ives irrelevantly.

'It's to lure us.'

'At least it keeps them busy.' The truth was, none of them had the faintest idea what to do next. They didn't have a rope and there was no way of getting one, that was the basic truth. There was a desperate pause before Nadire said, sounding frightened, 'What's that noise?' They listened, glad for a diversion. It was a rustling, hissing sort of sound in the undergrowth near them. 'I hope it's not a snake,' said Nadire, doubtfully.

Ruby had a sudden image of Cedric, the many coils of him, the increased height when he stood up, even though he left plenty of coils unreeled on the ground. Perhaps it *had* been him following them across the grassy plain . . .

'Cedric,' she called softly, trying to use Slate's voice. 'Is that you, Cedric? We need your help to rescue your friend and master.' She was pleading, pleading with a snake, but it seemed the only chance.

Cedric came slithering out of the darkness. He was unimaginably long. Twice as long, Ruby thought rather confusedly, as when she first saw him in London. He seemed heavier and stronger too. He looked at Ruby with intelligent, shining eyes. 'Follow us,' she whispered, staring nervously at his great mouth which was wide open enough to see a forked tongue. She thought she remembered Slate telling her that this jaw was hinged in such a way that he could swallow a chest of drawers. Maybe pretending to be a rope would offend his pride. But, at any rate, he followed them, the quietest of them all as they crawled back to the pit.

'We've got Cedric to help us,' whispered Ruby.

Slate was silent for a moment – giving thanks, Ruby presumed. 'Good man, Cedric,' he whispered eventually, adding with new anxiety, 'Lee's still asleep, so go easy. If she wakes up suddenly and sees a snake, she might scream.'

Ruby, Nadire and St Ives each looked nervously at the enemy camp. They could not see the black figures any more. Perhaps they were eating. Or perhaps they were on their way towards them . . . 'Hurry! Hurry!' said Nadire. And they all agreed.

If Ruby had pictured holding on to Cedric's tail while Slate hung on to his head and they all hauled him up, she soon found out how wrong she was. In less than a second, the snake had shot down into the pit, coiled round Slate, picked him up and placed him with them on the edge.

'Quelle force!' exclaimed St Ives.

'Sssh,' said Slate, severely. Then added in surprised tones, 'I guess he's grown since coming to the Island?' They noticed he was trembling, although they liked to feel it was from relief, not fear. For a moment, they had forgotten Lee, until they realised Cedric had disappeared down the pit once more. Crouching, they peered nervously over the edge. What they managed to make out in the darkness made them even more nervous. Lee, already wrapped in the snake's coils, was beginning to mutter. It was impossible to tell whether her eyes were open or not but she certainly gave every indication of waking up and they all dreaded just how she'd react when she did open them.

'Aaahhh! Aieeee! H-e-e-e-l-p!' Suspended by Cedric at the top of the pit, Lee's timing was perfect. Her screams couldn't possibly have been louder. Behaving with commendable calm, Cedric dropped her into the midst of the others who did their best to smother her, sit on her, clasp their hands over her mouth, or shut her up in any way possible.

'Aaaieee!' She had wriggled free with the strength of ten, and was screaming even louder. I'm afraid no one felt the slightest pity for her, or even considered that someone who had been kidnapped, drugged and thrown into a pit had every right to be scared out of their wits when they woke up to find themselves held aloft by a snake. How could she have known he had come, not to threaten her, but to save her?

'You're just a ratty stowaway!' hissed Ruby, viciusly grabbing one of Lee's arms while Nadire grabbed the other.

'You're a fille malheureuse,' squeaked St Ives.

'Like you don't deserve rescuing!' spat out Slate.

'Oooooh! Ugh! Owwww!' Lee screamed even louder. Short of bashing her on the head and knocking her unconscious, there was clearly no way of stopping her.

Almost resignedly, Ruby thought that Lee had always been good at making the kind of racket that drew attention to her. All of them (except Lee, of course) looked towards the camp.

Sure enough, they could see black silhouetted figures once more, but now they were on their feet and heading their way.

Chapter Fifteen

Seeing the truth

They could have run. There was just time to head away fast, dragging Lee with them, and hide in the undergrowth. Except it wasn't so dark any more. While they had been rescuing Slate and Lee, a pale dawn had begun to light the sky. It would soon be brighter than the lights from the camp in front of them. And anyway, they would never have been able to persuade the still shrieking Lee. But most important of all, they just didn't want to run. They wanted to stand firm and see just who their enemies were. Who these Others were. Without speaking to each other, they all came to the same conclusion. They stood, they linked arms, bravely they stared at their attackers.

'There're far more of them than I expected,' muttered Ruby. She tried to count, but St Ives was quicker.

'Vingt-et-un. Twenty-one.'

Twenty-one! It was impossible they could defend themselves against so many.

'Like that pit wasn't the greatest place,' murmured Slate, in case anyone was thinking he should have been left there.

Suddenly, the light changed in the most startling and dramatic way. One minute everything looked pallid and misty so that shapes were almost harder to see than if there'd been no light at all, the next there were huge beams blazing from behind them and directed like spotlights on the advancing group. At exactly the same moment, there was a new loud sound which, if Ruby hadn't known it was impossible, she would have described as applause, as a large group of people clapping enthusiastically.

'They clap!' exclaimed Nadire.

'They clap hands!' cried St Ives, as if, thought Ruby, quite mesmerised by the sound, they would clap anything else.

'Like . . .' Slate paused as if he'd lost his breath, 'who are they?'

'Well, if you ask me . . .' began Ruby because she could hardly believe what she was seeing.

'Cherie!' yelled St Ives. And he was quite correct.

There was Cherie, laughing and cheering. Frederick

and April, glittering and glamorous as ever, Raymond and his helpers plus the rest of the Audition for Life children. Now they were only a few yards away.

'Congratulations!' It was Frederick, striding forward to greet them first, with April at his side. They were both dressed in triumphant red and white streamers, like mediaeval pennants.

'You have passed your audition with flying colours.' April took up the message.

'You have withstood dangers of every sort,' Frederick continued. 'You have been hungry, sleepless, kidnapped, in fear of death: by gunfire, by spiders, by drowning, by nameless terrors.'

'You have never wavered.'

'You have been loyal to each other.' At this point, Ruby remembered her less than loyal feelings about Lee with some guilt. But at least she had not acted on them. She was still trying to get her head around the idea that everything that had happened to them in the last twenty-four hours had been planned, as a test.

'Does it mean we were never really in danger?' whispered Slate, obviously as bewildered as her. But then there was no time for questions as they found themselves surrounded by cheering fans and led, better and better, to where a huge feast – they had, of course, been smelling it for hours – had been prepared to celebrate their triumph.

Two hours later, Ruby still felt pretty bemused, but extremely proud and happy. She and Slate had eaten so much of their favourite food that they were only just managing to stay awake. 'I've been meaning to ask you something,' Slate mumbled sleepily.

'What?'

'Meant to ask you earlier. What ever have you done with your hair?'

'I've mislaid it,' Ruby smiled into the darkness, 'in a place where it will never be found again.'

'Cool. Much better without. You look almost, like normal.'

'Thanks. Slate?

'Uhm.'

'Do you think we get off the island now?'

But she was asleep before she heard the answer.

CHAPTER SIXTEEN

At sea

The rocking was just what rocking should be; gentle, reassuring, rhythmical. Ruby hoped it would never stop, that she would never need to wake up. But her eyes were determined to open. She looked around. She, Slate, Nadire and Lee were all lying on bunk beds. Above the beds were round portholes, through which she could see deep blue sky.

'Enfin!' She turned her head and saw St Ives at the door. 'Wake up. We're at sea. Voilà!'

He swept his hand to the outside world and Ruby caught a glimpse of glittering waves as blue as the sky. She found herself dragged up by St Ives and led to the deck at the stern of the ship. He held on to the rail and pointed. 'That's the last of the Island. The end. Lee and Nadire and Slate will not see it.'

Ruby peered. The island was so small that she could only make out a sort of dark triangular shape as it rose to the mountain peak. She shuddered as she recalled their terrible journey through it.

'Can you see it?' asked St Ives curiously.

' 'Course I can.'

'But you're not wearing tes lunettes.'

Ruby smiled. She didn't even bother to point out that ever since her glasses had disappeared in the flood, she'd been seeing better than ever.

'It was cutting my hair that did it,' she said, laughing. It was, after all, as good an explanation as any.

'Why didn't you wake us?' Slate and Nadire and Lee arrived to join them on deck. They all stared at the water rushing away from them, at the white froth of the wake and the tiny dot of the island.

Ruby wanted to ask Slate and Lee about their experiences in captivity. The party to celebrate their triumph had been far too much fun to spoil it with horrible stories. But now they were on their way home – at least she assumed they were on their way home – perhaps the moment had come. She took Slate's arm. 'You know when the guns went off, when you were kidnapped . . .' Ruby faltered to a stop. His dark eyes were looking at her so oddly, almost blankly.

'Guns?' he repeated. 'What about guns?' His blankness

gave way to a kind of aggression. 'I hate guns.'

'I know. I mean, we all do . . .'

'If it hadn't been for guns . . .' Slate bent closer over the dark water as if somewhere in its depths there was a message for him. He straightened abruptly. 'My dad nearly killed a man with a gun. He's inside. In prison. Has been for four years.'

Ruby listened with horror. She saw that Nadire and St Ives were listening too and wore the same expression of shock.

'They were fighting. And this other man had a knife. They'd been drinking. That's what my brother blames. The drink. But I blame the gun. It was self-defence but that's not how the court saw it.'

As Ruby wondered what to say, Nadire stepped forward. 'Your dad's a rough man, yes?'

Slate turned away. Nadire took his arm. 'I know about rough men. About guns. I told you about my brother being killed and my father and brother did things I do not like. They tried to hide it from me. I say they good men who did bad things because bad things had been done to them.'

'But that makes them,' Slate paused, 'like bad too.' His voice was only a mumble.

'Yes, good and bad. Not all bad.' There was a long silence. Ruby saw the island had disappeared altogether.

'I always wanted my dad to be good, like a hero.' Slate was speaking so softly now they could hardly hear. 'But when I was in that pit, I knew he was bad like those masked men who took me. I hated them and I hated him.'

St Ives took hold of Slate's other hand. 'You're lucky. He lives.' There was a silence while they all remembered St Ives had neither mother nor father and very probably Nadire didn't either.

Then Slate burst out, 'I wish he wasn't alive! I wish he wasn't my dad! I wish he would be at least a bit good!' As he shouted, the boat gave a sharp jerk, shuddered wildly and all of a sudden the noise of the engine which had been in the background ever since they had woken stopped. Everything became completely silent, the boat, although still proceeding forward, began to slow down. Soon they would be drifting aimlessly.

Until this moment, none of them had given any thought as to who was crewing the boat. They just assumed they were roaring homewards, mission accomplished. Audition for Life completed. But now it struck them that their adventures might not be finished after all. With one accord, they dashed forward to the cabin which was near the bow of the boat. It was completely empty and the wheel was beginning to swing wildly.

'Grab it before we start going in circles!' cried Slate, his own problems forgotten, and, with St Ives' help, they got it under control.

Ruby, Nadire and Lee meanwhile, were trying to peer ahead through the cabin window. Whereas the view from the stern had been all blue sky and blue water, a cloudless view of tropical warmth, the view ahead was cloudy, quite dark, with the waves turbulent and a dark greeny-black.

'I think,' said Ruby, tentatively, 'there might be land in front of us. Even quite near.'

'You can't possibly tell,' said Lee rudely. She hadn't, Ruby noticed, managed to say one nice thing about her new look hair. Of all of them, she seemed least changed by their adventures except, Ruby noticed, when she was around St Ives she suddenly became very nice and protective.

Ignoring her, Ruby and Nadire went out of the cabin to the bow. It had begun to rain and a mist, rising from the sea, merged with the low cloud. The boat, without its engine to keep it steady, was bucketing round in the waves so that they had to hang on tight to the railings.

'There is land,' confirmed Nadire. 'Look at those birds.' Dark gulls shrieked and flapped above their heads, occasionally swooping low enough to make the girls duck. Ruby felt newly grateful for her close-cropped curls.

'Well, let's hope we can reach it without an engine.'

'We can row,' said Nadire, shivering. They both realised at the same time that they were extremely cold, freezing and wet in their tropical island clothes, and they hurried back into the cabin.

'There's land not far ahead,' they announced.

'We can't get the engine started. It turns over but doesn't fire. We've probably run out of fuel,' Slate

132

frowned anxiously. 'With a wind like this we could be blown anywhere.'

'Oi! Come out here!' It was St Ives calling from the deck. They could see him, face almost hidden by wet curls, frantically waving and shouting. As soon as they reached him, he took them to a bulky shape on deck covered by a thick tarpaulin. 'It's un canot de sauvetage,' he said. 'A life-boat. If we can put it in the water, we can row ourselves to shore.'

'And abandon this motor-boat?' asked Slate.

'There's a storm coming up,' Lee pointed out.

Ruby thought that was the first sensible thing Lee had said.

'I don't think we have any choice.'

Their numb and slippery fingers made hard work of the ropes holding down the tarpaulin, but eventually they had it off. 'Hey, look at this,' Slate was poking under the front boards, 'Our backpacks are here. And guess what else!'

Ruby looked and saw Cedric's head lolling sleepily out of the top of Slate's bag. He didn't seem afraid of the wind and waves. Briefly, she wondered about Aurora before returning to the matter in hand. Secretly, she was was beginning to have images of the sinking of the *Titanic*.

'How do we launch the boat?' she asked.

'There's a machine,' said St Ives in a competent voice.

How they managed to launch the boat which, though small, was very heavy, amazed all of them. But in a matter of ten minutes or so, there it was, bobbing down below them, knocking against the side of their smart launch.

'Go!' shouted St Ives who seemed to have taken temporary command. The truth was that none of the others had any idea how to deal with the sea – let alone a rough, threatening sea.

'Jump!' called St Ives. And they jumped, making the boat rock so madly that it was a wonder they didn't fall straight out again.

'Row!' screamed St Ives, because it was very noisy down among the waves and they were in danger of smashing against the motor boat.

They rowed, two to an oar, Slate and Nadire, Lee and Ruby. They hoped they were going in the right direction – if there was a right direction. St Ives acted as cox, ordering, 'À gauche. More on the left oar. À droit. More on the right,' as if he could actually see something which they all secretly doubted. At least they were warm again. Soon, rather more importantly, there was a new roaring sound ahead, as if waves were breaking against hard surfaces.

'Don't run us on to rocks!' yelled Slate.

Ruby thought St Ives could hardly choose where he ran them. She could imagine only too vividly their little boat being smashed into smithereens and them with it.

'I pray,' whispered Nadire.

'Pray for a port!' screamed St Ives. Above him, the gulls, which had followed the little boat, screamed even louder.

They began to find it harder and harder to row, their muscles aching, the oars bouncing off the water as often as they cut through it. The roaring noise got so loud it was completely deafening, while the heavy spray made them blind to everything but a turbulent darkness. The darkness increased until they were surrounded in a blackness so profound that they couldn't even see each other's faces.

It feels as if I am unconscious, thought Ruby. Perhaps I am about to die or even dead already.

They all had this same strange sensation. They felt as if their eyes were shut even though they knew they were open. Gradually they became aware that they were enveloped in total calm, peace, serenity, an oily blackness that was above and below them. They were still in the boat, still on the water but other than that, everything was different.

'The storm's gone,' said Ruby, trying to keep the trembling relief from her voice. She had nearly exclaimed, 'I'm alive!' Now she could see her friends' faces again.

'It's night-time,' said Nadire, looking dreamily up at the sky. 'Look at the stars. I can see Orion and Venus. I wonder where the rain went.'

'St Ives has saved our lives,' announced Lee, and no one contradicted her. He was a hero.

They all lay back and looked up at the sky as the boat drifted lazily. Now that the screeching gulls had gone, the only sound was the faint slap of water on the side of the boat, until Ruby heard an even gentler and more reassuring noise above her head. She opened her eyes wider and saw a white shape fluttering against the darkness. 'It's Aurora,' she said in a satisfied voice. 'Things always go well when Aurora arrives.'

'Perhaps we are in a bay,' suggested St Ives.

'It's a river,' Slate peered through the darkness. 'Like a very wide cool river. Maybe we're on the Amazon or the Nile or the Bramaputra.'

Ruby smiled to herself. She recognised this list from the longest rivers in the World section of their school atlas. Yet, after their recent experiences, anything did seem possible.

'It's too cold,' said Lee, a little bleakly. 'I think we're back in England.'

The stars were so many and so bright now that they could see each other's faces, all wondering, searching for banks to the river, for palm trees or jungles or buildings.

'It does feel dank, just the way England feels dank.' Actually, Ruby felt she'd had quite enough of adventures in mysterious foreign parts.

'Let's row,' suggested Slate, 'and see where we get to.'

So they began to row again, slowly now because they were tired and there seemed no immediate danger.

'Faster!' commanded St Ives.

'You're not rowing and you don't have blisters on your hands,' pointed out Slate bitterly. They both seemed ready to have a good argument until Ruby interrupted them.

'I think this river's in a big city. Look at the buildings.

Look at the street lights. Look at the traffic. Look at the people!'

They all looked. They must have been rowing diagonally across the river because now they were quite near the left bank and, just as Ruby had said, it was teeming with energetic city life.

'There's a bus!' exclaimed Lee.

'Does it have a number on it?' Slate craned sideways, making the boat rock dangerously. But the bus was going too fast. 'There's like somewhere we can land a few metres up.'

'I'm sure we're back in England.' St Ives' voice had become small and disheartened.

'Don't you want to be in England?' Lee asked him sympathetically while the others looked for a rope to moor the boat.

'Horrible school,' answered St Ives briefly, looking as if he were about to cry.

'They bully you, do they? It's an old-fashioned boarding school. I remember. You told us.'

'Please, can I stay with you all?' Suddenly, St Ives was clinging to Lee passionately. 'Come to your school?'

'Our school's not very nice . . .' began Lee before rethinking, 'but I guess it's a lot nicer than being an orphan stuck in the wilds on some cliff-top, surrounded by children who think you're a freak. You've been talking French much less recently,' she added, which Ruby could see from St Ives' miserable expression was not much of a consolation.

'Hey, you two! We're landing! Shake a leg!' It was Slate yelling.

'We think we're home,' Ruby mouthed the words with enormous satisfaction, before looking at Nadire guiltily. Where was her home?

CHAPTER SEVENTEEN

Home

They landed on an unlit jetty very like the one Ruby, Slate and Lee had first set out from. There was the same air of mild threat, garbage blown by the wind, a dog barking somewhere, tall buildings without windows or lighting, probably, but not certainly, unused.

'I feel as if I'm on the set for a thriller.' Lee didn't look as if she liked the idea.

'I've had enough thrills for one lifetime,' agreed Ruby.

'On va à pied?' asked St Ives which no one understood.

'Now you're in England, you'll have to speak English,' said Ruby severely and St Ives moved closer to Lee.

'We could, like walk?' suggested Slate.

'But where from to?' asked Nadire.

' "Where to?" ' corrected St Ives, priggishly, after which no one could think of anything to say. Instead they went up to the deserted road and leaned against the parapet looking down at the dark river. The boat, which they had tied up, bobbed gently in the water like a docile pet.

Suddenly there was the very loud noise of a large vehicle approaching extremely fast. Ruby crouched down as if she feared a tank with guns trained on them. She had time to notice everybody else was doing the same, except St Ives who was small enough already.

'It's a bus!' Slate bellowed. They looked and saw that indeed it was a large red bus, very like, if not the same one, that had delivered Ruby, Slate and stowaway Lee to the jetty in the first place. It seemed like a hundred years ago, but, if the truth be told, none of them had any idea of how long they'd been away. Their only concern was to get on the bus, although as before, it was completely empty and the driver, a young man with a thick beard, seemed remarkably uninterested in their destination or, luckily for them, the fact that they had no money to pay their fares.

'City centre,' he said, laconically and when Nadire asked, blushing rather, 'What city?' he didn't even bother to answer.

'Write your school address here,' he said, pushing a paper and pen under the glass partition. So Ruby wrote down the name and address of their school and that, they agreed without discussing it, would do for Nadire and St Ives too. They were part of the group now.

They climbed upstairs pushing each other in their haste, hurrying to the front so that they could see where they were going. The bus had already started with a jerk and was now rushing through the darkness.

'From the boat,' said Ruby carefully, 'we could see traffic and lights and people. But now there is nothing.'

As if on cue, they turned the corner round a high black building and found themselves faced by a line of stationary traffic, waiting for the lights to change. They were all too amazed to speak. Here was the real world.

'I . . . wicked . . . hey, man, I like know this street,' stuttered Slate.

'Me too!' rejoiced Lee and gave St Ives a hug.

It struck Ruby that Nadire and St Ives had no idea where they were and must be feeling very anxious and discombobulated. Nadire was sitting beside her, staring straight ahead.

'Where is your refugee . . .' she paused while she tried to find the right word, '. . . your refugee house?' Ruby asked her awkwardly, wondering why she'd never asked the question before.

In the neon bus lighting, Nadire's face looked pale and strained. She stared sideways out of the window and spoke with her face still turned away. 'I suppose your parents will be wondering where you are?' she asked.

'My mother,' Ruby touched her shoulder. 'Just my mother. My father left ages ago.' The lights changed and the bus dashed on.

'My aunt who is in this country doesn't want a daughter. She doesn't want me. She wants me to be gone forever.'

A sudden extraordinary idea struck Ruby. Extraordinary perhaps, but so good she couldn't think why she hadn't thought of it before. 'Oh, Nadire, you could come and live with me! My mother works all day. I'm on my own so much. I so need a sister!'

Nadire looked at her with her big serious eyes. Ruby could see she was trying to see whether Ruby really meant it. Then she put out her hand. She smiled. Their hands locked and a pact had been made.

'We're on the road to school, you know!' Slate was off his seat peering excitedly through the bus window. 'Look for yourselves! There's the post office and the betting shop . . .'

'But it's night-time,' pointed out Lee, not sounding at all pleased at the idea.

'I think day comes?' Nadire spoke so quietly that it took a moment for her words to sink in.

'But like the sun only went down when we got into the boat.'

'That can't be more than a few hours ago,' added Lee.

'The sky is lighter,' said Nadire briefly. She was right. The street lamps were dimmer, the car headlights less bright and the sky no longer black.

'Morning comes,' continued Nadire, turning to Ruby. 'What do you do in the morning?'

'Go to school,' said Ruby and, for some reason, she found herself giggling.

*   *   *

The bus stopped, not near the school at a normal bus stop, but directly outside the gates where pupils were streaming in just as if it were a regular school day. Ruby, Slate and Lee watched in a dazed sort of way.

'All out!' called the conductor.

Slowly they trooped down the stairs. Ruby caught a glimpse of herself reflected in the window and realised just how odd she looked, and how different, no glasses, little hair, dirty backpack. Bedraggled holiday T-shirt and jeans, definitely no uniform. And yet it seemed natural that they were heading for school. She looked at the others and saw they looked just as odd; Lee's usually smooth dark hair was a complete tangle and Slate's jeans were filthy with several large holes. She wanted to say, 'We can't go in like this,' but instead found herself taking Nadire's arm and insisting in extraordinarily firm tones, 'You must come in with us!'

'Right-on,' agreed Slate, taking St Ives' hand. Ruby saw this with some amazement. After all, Slate at school never mixed with any but the coolest of the cool. St Ives, with his ragamuffin appearance and French vocabulary, was very much un-cool. And for Slate to hold a younger boy's hand was verging, in terms of reputation, on the suicidal. It was less odd to see Lee holding St Ives' other hand.

Nevertheless, there they were, mixing with the morning rush into school and, strangely, causing no odd looks. Instinctively, as on so many mornings before,

Ruby looked at her watch. Eight fifty-five. She did a double take. 'My watch is working again!'

Slate turned over his wrist. 'Mine too.' Clearly, they really were back in the real world.

'I think,' said Lee slowly, 'our best bet is to go straight to the headmaster. We have to sort out St Ives and Nadire.'

Ruby and Slate looked at each other. This was a bold suggestion. No one *chose* to see the headmaster. He was punishment time.

'Like, OK,' agreed Slate reluctantly. Nadire and St Ives expressed no opinion on the matter. In fact they hadn't spoken since leaving the bus. Ruby wondered vaguely if Nadire had lost the use of the English which she had picked up so quickly.

As they approached the headmaster's door, it opened wide and a teacher with a clipboard hurried out. Before it could close again, Mr Harpsden spotted the approaching group. He was a loud-voiced man, who favoured repetition. His welcoming bellow echoed down the corridor, 'Come in, come in, you lot! I've been waiting for you!'

They looked at each other, bewildered. How could he have known they were coming? And yet there was no one else in the corridor.

'Good! Good!' He leant forward over his desk as they crowded in. 'Let's see now. Nadire and St Ives isn't it? Well. Well. And I see you've already met your sponsors, although I didn't expect you, Lee. Are you part of this gang of ruffians?' He looked at her questioningly.

Lee stared at her feet, blushing. 'I guess I just tagged along.'

'Good. Good! All hands to the tiller. So. So. No school today. Off home and clean yourself up! The paperwork will take me all morning to sort out. Well. Well. I welcome you to your new school, Nadire and St Ives. Now. Now. What are you staring at? I've things to do. Off. Off! I happen to know your mother's taken a day off work, Ruby. Out. Out. And your father's back home, Slate. I had him here yesterday, standing just where you are. Talking about getting out of a deep hole. A black pit, he described it. Making a change of direction. Well. Well. Don't let's talk about his past! The future's the thing. Yes. Yes. I agreed with him. Change! We can all change or we're dead. Off you go! What are you waiting for?'

Nadire took a step forward. 'I have no home, please sir.'

'Didn't I explain? No. No. Yes. Yes. Your home is with Ruby. Ruby's home is your home now. Her mother your mother. She's looking forward to meeting you. Says she always wanted another child. A taller child. Ahem.'

'And me, monsieur?' St Ives took a hesitant step forward. 'Where is my home?'

'Ah. Yes.' The headmaster looked down at a piece of paper in front of him. 'Didn't I explain that either? I guess you'd like to go with, like Slate here.' The headmaster boomed a laugh. 'Boys together. But the authorities wouldn't have that, not with his father's past.

They have to be convinced about change. Deep dark holes, pits, whatever . . . But your home is very close, a very nice, respectable family called Tompkinson . . .'

'But my name's Tompkinson!' Lee burst out.

The headmaster looked surprised and then nodded vigorously. 'Indeed. Indeed. That's why you were tagging along. Very modest way of putting it. Good. Good. That's settled then. On your way now.'

They walked back along the corridor, which was quiet now as the other children had gone into their classrooms. They were too dazed to talk much. So much seemed to have changed in such a short time. Ruby glanced at the notice board. She did not expect to see more than the usual, 'Lost and Found' notices, but wanted to pay homage at the place where all their adventures had started.

'Do you remember that weird card . . . ?'

She turned to Slate but he was staring past her, directly at the notice board, eyes nearly popping out of his head. So she turned back again.

There, right in the middle of the notice board was a large multi-coloured card, although it was more like a screen because the words were flashing in and out. She read out loud:

'CONGRATULATIONS ON COMPLETING THE FIRST STAGE OF THE AUDITION FOR LIFE!'

'First stage?' repeated Slate in a questioning tone.

'WATCH THIS SPACE,' flashed the card before very slowly fading, until there was the merest hint of rainbow colours on the card which gradually changed into a notice announcing fines for dropping litter.

'Home,' said Ruby, suddenly feeling very tired. She turned to Nadire. 'It's not that I'm against a second stage, but I just need time to recover from the first.'

'Like cool,' agreed Slate and they all smiled at each other.

THE MEMORY PRISONER

Thomas Bloor

Maddie stood for a while, staring out into the street. She felt, as she always did when confronted by a open door, as if she was standing on the edge of a precipice overlooking a bottomless ocean . . .

Maddie is fifteen and overweight. She hasn't left the house for thirteen years, since her grandfather disappeared.

Burying her memories, Maddie can't face her deepest fears. Until her brother's life is in danger – and she must leave her familiar prison behind, or lose him for good . . .

A Fidler Award-winning novel

'Subversive, funny and imaginative' *The Observer*

'Bizarrely comic' *The Guardian*

'Moving, alarming and funny' Jan Mark, *TES*

THE IVY CROWN

Gill Vickery

'*I wish I could see my mother again — just once — and tell her I'm sorry I didn't keep my promise.*'

Staying with their father in a bizarre Gothic house in a sinister woodland, Megan and her younger brother, Brand, are struggling to come to terms with their grief and guilt over their mother's recent death.

But the house harbours its own secrets, and soon Megan and Brand find themselves on a quest to put right the mistakes of the past — but only if they choose to accept a dangerous bargain . . .

A Fidler Award-winning novel